The Sky is Falling
Lorenza Mazzetti

Published by
Another Gaze Editions

Table of Contents

4

Foreword

Ali Smith

This welcome reissue and new translation into English, of Lorenza Mazzetti's first novel, *Il cielo cade* (1962) could not be more timely. Mazzetti, who died in Rome in 2020 at the age of 92, was a spirited and brilliant pioneer and artist across several aesthetic genres. She was a writer of fiction, polemic and criticism; a painter; a seasoned Roman street theatre puppeteer (!); and a hugely influential filmmaker. As a filmmaker she was and still is far too unknown here in the UK, even though she was one of the four seminal filmmakers (and the only woman; the others were Tony Richardson, Lindsay Anderson and Karel Reisz) who formed the massively influential mid-twentieth century movement known as Free Cinema, which altered the possibilities for British film narrative and film art.

Her life history is remarkable. Lorenza Mazzetti first came to the UK at the start of the fifties when she was in her early twenties, as part of an initiative to bring people from mainland Europe to help with work on British farms. She'd grown up in Italy; when her mother died not long after their birth, she and her twin sister Paola were left by their father in the care of friends and relatives and eventually ended up living with their father's sister, Cesarina Mazzetti, on a large farm and estate in the beautiful Tuscan *comune* of Rignano sull'Arno. Cesarina, known as Nina, was married to Robert Einstein, a cousin of Albert Einstein, and together they brought the Mazzetti girls up alongside their own two daughters, Anna Maria and Luce. During the Second World War the farm was requisitioned by the Nazi forces. In August 1944, when Italy had changed allegiance and the Allied forces were driving the Nazis into retreat, Wehrmacht officers arrived at the farm to arrest Robert Einstein. When they couldn't find him they murdered Nina, Anna Maria and Luce. He returned to find his wife and daughters dead; shortly afterwards, he took his own life.

The Mazzetti twins, then in their teens, only survived the massacre of the family because their name wasn't Einstein.

Wandering London numbly after the war, with the words 'undesirable alien' stamped by a British officer into her passport, searching for work and warding off a madness she couldn't articulate, Lorenza Mazzetti talked her way against the odds into a place at the Slade School of Art. In a cupboard in a corridor there one day she found a lot of film equipment. She 'borrowed' it all, gathered together a group of students, friends, people she met in passing, and began making immensely powerful, experimental and original films. These were largely influenced by the writings of Kafka, especially his *Metamorphosis*, which she revered as a text whose powerful accusation works against any tendency to become numbed towards or indifferent to injustice.

In her years here, which you can read about first hand in her *London Diaries* (Zidane Press, 2019), her own traumatic past began to dawn on her and this first novel is one of the earliest of her own powerful written acts of accusation against such indifference.

The Sky is Falling opens with its main character, Penny (a character notably much younger in her fictional form than Mazzetti was), being reprimanded for a dream. Penny is a small child in Second World War Italy: one who, along with all the other children

Ali Smith

at the village school, sings lovely fascist hymns at the top of her lungs about how all the children are the 'golden dawn' who'll 'make Italy greater forever-more', hearts full of love for Mussolini, as they warble like finches about the sacrifices they'd make for him. Penny and her sister Baby are 'poor orphans' living with the family of their well-off relatives on a wealthy estate. At school they daily dress and act as members of little militarised squads taught to love and obey Jesus, catechism and fascism in equal measure.

But when Penny dreams of a Virgin Mary as bald and smooth-headed as the helmeted Mussolini, then faithfully answers the homework essay question *what did you dream about last night* with what she *really* dreamt, her teacher's furious response to this dream – both laugh-out-loud funny and terrifyingly revealing about the conflation of religion and political powerplay – tells the reader everything. 'She made me bring her my exercise book and scratched an ugly red mark across the page.' Then the teacher slaps the child.

Blasphemy! The girls are poor relations living with the local well-off family. The family is not acceptable locally either. 'The Devil is in this little girl's house,' the village priest says about Penny. Still, she *can* be saved from Hell; even if she and her sister do have too foreign a surname for comfort, at least they've been baptised. But their beloved uncle? 'Condemned to eternal suffering.'

Penny wonders 'if the sun really was yellow or if it was yellow only for me. Perhaps Uncle, who was a Jew, saw it as blue or green...' But both girls know instinctually, with the open eyes of childhood, that identity is a wide-open possibility, and why wouldn't it be?

'Baby, don't you think it's strange you're not me?'
'What?'
'I love you so much that it seems impossible to me
that you're not me. I don't know what you are,
and you don't know what i am either.'
'You're Penny.'
'I feel like this tree. What do you feel like?'
Baby said she felt like the grasshopper we could
hear singing from somewhere nearby, and I said
I felt like that swallow in the sky, and we contin-
ued like this for a very long time.

One day Penny decides to get up early to get a good
look at a golden dawn. She climbs as high up a tree
as she can. Above the idyllic Tuscan landscape she
imagines she's a bird then spends the morning count-
ing the leaves on the tree. Beneath her, over at the
Villa, guests have arrived. These guests aren't the
usual house guests. They're Wehrmacht soldiers.
They seem nice. They play the piano, play chess with
Penny's uncle, occasionally wearily or lovingly join
in with some of the children's games.

The novel has already signalled that children's
games are revealing, that they – and the children
who play them – understand something about per-
formativity, lies and power, and that a knowledge of
something deeply unhealthy surfaces in the perfor-
mance. 'Where does it hurt?' a child pretending to be
a doctor asks a child pretending to be a society figure.
'Everywhere,' is the answer. 'Awful weather,' Baby
says looking at a bright blue sky, because that's the
kind of thing you're supposed to say. The child world
of this time and place is underscored with knowing
lies, self-hurt, self-punishment, above all an incipient

Ali Smith

violence, part hilarious, part profoundly chilling: 'I'd have to kill Rosa if I heard her say bad things about Benito Mussolini again,' the child declares. And then, as the story darkens, 'I began to feel nervous about going back downstairs without having successfully hanged myself.'

Is this funny? For the most part *The Sky is Falling* seems a darkly comic novel, sometimes laugh-out-loud funny, a fever dream of innocence and bewilderment. But the novel is saturated with a tension that surfaces in a melee of broken things, a rising hysteria that veers towards madness, a played-out ritualising of human hurt and cruelty. Written in small, short, perfectly formed sections that ape something slight, something dismissible, only child-sized, it analyses with painful sharpness the enmeshment of political fervour with religious fervour. It tracks the political, social and historical power games alongside the children's games, marks the coercion, control and bullying that supports a political power system and a belief system, and tells us straight, unfiltered, what humans can and will do – and have done – to one another and themselves. It is full of love, yet organised hate ricochets throughout; throughout, the children fear the threat of Hell, then this book, with its small group of children, their arms stretched high, 'red from the effort' of trying to 'hold up the sky', reveals what hell literally is. Its visions turn into something searing and real. Its end delivers a truth. This is no dream, and something more than a novel.

More than any of Mazzetti's other written works, *The Sky is Falling* is about the routing – but simultaneously the preservation, the honouring – of innocents. In her next fiction, a sister novel to this one, *Con rabbia* (*Rage*, 1963), Mazzetti writes, 'I couldn't live in calmness and boredom any more. My hand has touched blood and tragedy and I know that while boredom was dozing, reality was preparing the apocalypse.' But with this strange, funny, sad, deft, terrifying, and finally stunning first novel, Lorenza Mazzetti began her written quest into truth, into the question of how to tell it so it will not be lost, cannot be buried, above all might be understood in all its ramification, all its loss.

With the form she found for this fiction, indifference isn't possible. In it, the innocence of the people lost to and touched by this real tragedy, and by extention all innocents and innocence, survive the tragedy simultaneously, rise out of it, truth told, truth known.

Ali Smith

After the fall

Francesca Massarenti

Cosa può fare un bambino per cambiare le regole o le scelte dei grandi? Niente.
[What can a child do to change the rules or the choices made by grownups? Nothing.]
—Lorenza Mazzetti, *Una vita, mille vite* (2021)

*

In the last pages of her *London Diaries* (*Diario londinese*, 2014), Lorenza Mazzetti recalls how she came to write her first novel, *The Sky is Falling* (*Il cielo cade*), fifty years earlier. She remembers an afternoon spent sitting at the bar of Hotel Corallo in Sperlonga – a seaside town halfway between Rome and Naples – glancing between the blank pages of her notebook and the waters of the Tyrrhenian Sea. Suddenly she writes the opening line to *The Sky is Falling*: "*Pensierino*: raccontate che cosa avete fatto oggi" ["*Exercise:* What did you do at school today?"]. Then she crumples up and tosses away the handwritten sheet:

> *Non era serio parlare di una tragedia così grande in questo modo, come se fossi una bambina.*
> [It's not serious to write this way about such a great tragedy, as if I were a child.]

The novel that Mazzetti will eventually write is, up until its last pages, a joyful memoir of countryside living and childhood discovery in Fascist Italy in which she recounts the execution of her adoptive family in 1944 by a group of German soldiers. A friend picks up the discarded page, reads it, and urges her to adopt the same style for a whole book, to write in a way that is deliberately unserious: "È proprio lì la sua bellezza. Non è mica un saggio sul Nazismo! Vero?" ["That's its beauty. It's not an essay about Nazism, is it?"]. Their exchange sheds some light on whether Mazzetti's mock ingénue tone came naturally or was adopted deliberately. The answer is that it is likely a little of both, but this isn't much help when it comes to contending with the narrative that is *The Sky is Falling*. In recent years there has been a surge in women's life writing – in terms of reappraisal, (re)translation and understanding of the craft – though one which has not yet considered Mazzetti's work. Other popular literary life story projects – such as Tove Ditlevsen's youth memoirs, translated as *The Copenhagen Trilogy*, or Annie Ernaux's corpus of "auto-socio-biography" – build on an affective reconstruction of bygone times which is consistently underpinned by the author's awareness of the extent to which writing can bend and warp events. In this kind of writing, both memoirist and reader are encouraged to keep their emotional involvement in check, lest they mistake a subjective, slanted account for a clear-headed deposition. Mazzetti, however, does not seem to be concerned with issues of authorial objectivity, nor to fear hyperbole and magnification in her writing. She seems quite at ease in a form that is her own: a memoir that *feels* like a novel.

Mazzetti, who was in her mid-thirties at the time of writing, uses simple, childish language to craft a childlike thought process on the page. The effect created is that of the illusion of a living scene, a fairy tale performed out loud. It is as if her recollection does not stem solely from individual knowledge: rather,

Francesca Massarenti

her catalysing style evokes the accumulated energy of myth. The raw bundle of memories is purportedly Mazzetti's own, yet the beauty of *The Sky is Falling* comes from its all-encompassing voice. The novel is told from Penny's point of view, but at the same time it gathers up an entire range of dialogue and song, cries and gossip, radio bulletins, the everyday nursery rhymes, anthems and prayers uttered by the people around her. Everything is absorbed and yet very little is fully digested. Swift, concise sentences keep at bay the relentless tide of information and action that crashes up against a young girl's life. The effect created is one of ethical formlessness: Penny's suspicion has not yet been honed, and though contradiction and paradox weigh on their lives she cannot understand them – nothing feels bad until it hurts. Adult reactions are baffling and unexplained, whether they are responses to run-of-the-mill annoyances or gushing radio propaganda. Children play at war in the courtyard and 'Adam and Eve' in the woods; they voice fullthroated, joyful pledges to the "Fascist revolution" which are as innocent as their impromptu exorcism ritual against a rooster who they decide is the devil. Within all of this we are shown the relentless building of one girl's moral code as her days collide with the realities of the world she must inhabit. Above all, Mazzetti lays bare the workings of a young and relatively unformed mind. This is also proof of her malleability. Her reminiscences are highly controlled and non-nostalgic: for the story to emerge as devoid of adult hindsight or learned wisdom, Mazzetti must commit to reviving them in writing in a way that mirrors the intensity of emotion felt at the time.

Doing so is a very serious endeavour. Mazzetti does not so much as look back on her childhood as forgo her adult self and the serenity of established identity to re-inhabit an earlier shape that lacks the crucial combination of experience, knowledge and detachment that gives sense to one's flaring energy.

The exploration and uncovering of past personal trauma via biographical writing is a well-trodden path for Italian authors coming to terms with postwar, post-Fascist Italy. Natalia Ginzburg's *Family Lexicon* (*Lessico famigliare*) was published two years after *The Sky is Falling*. Usually treated as a novel, Ginzburg's *Family Lexicon* reads like a taxonomy of beloved family vignettes, each thematically and narratively chained to the next regardless of linear chronology. While Ginzburg herself is present, her voice is not self-centring: she allows her figure to slip into the background as she recollects the eccentricities of her relatives and scarcely seems to allow herself more prominence even in the latter part of the book, when she recalls the anxiety-filled days of her husband's incarceration, torture and eventual death in 1944. Ultimately affection trumps grief in both works, each displaying a preference for showing the best and most immediate over a reflective experience of nostalgia or an *a posteriori* meditation on grief. Each writer, however, approaches the task of preserving their lost family's words, gestures and moods differently. Where Ginzburg maintains sobriety and full control – she must not give into an excess of feeling as she ties together scraps and snippets because she must preserve her memories in as pure and unadulterated a form as possible in

Francesca Massarenti

case she needs them later – Mazzetti gives herself more leeway to indulge in exuberance, playful daydreaming and boastful storytelling.

Regardless of style, both writers imbue their stories with the same drive: the fierce, animal need to keep themselves alive as things around them crumble, people disappear and the heaviest of powers exerts a stranglehold that tightens daily. Complexities are expected to arise whenever factual events are turned into narrative material, and in Mazzetti's case authenticity twists into something even more salient than first-hand testimony, becoming one with significance and cautionary intent. If we concede that manifest fictionality does not undermine the authority of Mazzetti's biographical perspective, it nevertheless appears to be obtrusive enough to impact its tone, as well as to manipulate the genre of the work. There are passages that turn *The Sky is Falling* from novel into fable, where monsters cast shadows that the young and inexperienced heroine must recognise in order to proceed with caution. Yet barely has the heroic journey started before it comes to a crushing halt. Penny's coming of age remains hazy: her family's death and uncle's suicide force her to become intimate with the deepest of sorrows, a pain so profound that it almost prevents her learning anything from it. Penny gapes at the destruction left behind by the monster, but as of yet cannot confront it.

In the books that follow, Penny will thrash around the world without ever seeming to come to a clear understanding of herself. Messiness as subject matter, however, should be distinguished from the disjointedness of its telling. It is risky to theorise a lack of planning in Mazzetti's trilogy. *The Sky is Falling* is followed by two adolescent anarcho-fantasist escape memoirs, *Con rabbia* (1963; translated into English by Isabel Quigly in 1965 as *Rage*) and *Uccidi il padre e la madre* (*Killing the Father and the Mother*, untranslated), and later by her *London Diaries*, yet the consistent repetition of themes, moods, and sometimes even turns of phrases does suggest a tendency for redundancy that a careful outline or attentive editor might have amended. Indeed, it is difficult to read the works in sequence, and given Mazzetti's often explicit recycling – which in a few instances even verges of self-plagiarism – continuity may not have even been envisaged. The chasms between each literary release seemingly operate as a sort of buffer space that enables the repurposing of well-sedimented material. Mazzetti's hesitation to clarify her literary intentions – an attitude that may also reflect the contemporary absence of a critical vocabulary with which to describe literary forms such as auto-fiction, biographical nonfiction, and so on – both outside and inside her work contributes to the feeling that reading it means having to cope directly with raw, traumatic personal experience, despite the layers of constructedness provided by the consistent stylisation, recycling and use of childish tropes.

At the time (though this is arguably still true today) both Italian publishing and its surrounding critical apparatus struggled to notice (and hence to market) books that fell on the gradient between literary genres. There were novels – *romanzi* – and then there were essayistic texts – *saggi* – usually serious in tone and expansive in their execution. Mutual contamination was discouraged at best and ignored at

Francesca Massarenti

worst, and this was followed by a forced re-shelving of the text in question beneath one of the aforementioned labels. Mazzetti chose, or perhaps found herself, naturally inhabiting a hybrid writing mode. Yet she was publishing in an environment that, given the sleekness of the result and her sidelining of historical accuracy, firmly characterised her experiments as novelistic matter. It makes little sense to evaluate *The Sky is Falling* and Mazzetti's subsequent literary efforts as examples of auto-fiction or creative biography ahead of their time – Mazzetti simply wrote what she knew in the style that suited her best. Yet the cohesive characterisation and controlled narrative architecture we often demand of novels and the deep self-reflection and insightful detachment we expect from autobiographical writing ultimately inhibit one another in her writing. Mazzetti deploys the freedom of invention allowed in fiction writing but grafts her work on truth claims that seemingly exonerate her from the need to provide her readers with a foundation that might keep her story from spinning out of control. The disaster at the end, moreover, seems indissolubly tied to motive of the telling itself, thus complicating the possibility for the crafting of an aesthetic experience independent of its duty to bear testimony, and therefore valuable in its own right. What remains unanswerable is whether the presentation of Mazzetti's works to the world as novels – perhaps the only form that would guarantee her readers – undercuts or perhaps even erases the real events at the heart of its narrative endeavour. *The Sky is Falling* sits in a middle zone between genre expectations and narrative conventions, and because of this it often fails to satisfy any of them, for all that it reinvigorates the potentialities of inscribing the self and its truths into a written text.

The Sky is Falling opens with the word *pensierino*, which means a small thought, a whole genre in and of itself for Italian schoolchildren. *Pensierini* are brief statements that pupils are required to write down in order to practise their calligraphy, monitor their spelling, experiment with proper syntax and ultimately to try and craft a meaningful sentence. Before you get to full compositions, *temi*, Italian schools require you to learn how to string together your thoughts. "What did you do at school today?" is Mazzetti's assigned homework; her task is that of paying attention to one's early life as it is being lived. Yet most of life is raw material unsuitable for homework, such as young Penny's dreams about a bald Madonna whose shiny features weirdly resemble those of Mussolini's own haloed effigy. It is the late thirties and Catholicism and national politics are presented as integrated practices to children like Penny and her sister Baby, trained – along with their whole generation – as *piccole italiane*, child fascists whose chirping prayers implore the divine protection of their Duce. However, life outside of state institutions offers the children a better alternative: adopted by their Aunt Katchen and Uncle Wilhelm after the death of their parents, Penny and Baby are granted the same privileges and cultural advantages as their cousins Marie and Annie. At the Villa multiple languages are spoken fluently, meals are prepared by the cook, Elsa, and the girls are picked up after school by their butler-chauffeur, Cosimo, in a velour-cushioned car. Private violin lessons are offered by Mister Pit, a family friend, and games of chess are played. Despite plentiful cultural and artistic stimulation at the Villa – which themselves embody the set of values and tastes that make up the highbrow culture of the period – the children cannot resist the lure of wilder pastimes. Behind the Villa there is a thick grove of old laurels where the sisters prefer to spend their afternoons dangling from tree branches, spurred on by their barely literate buddies, the peasant children Lea, Pasquetta, Zeffirino and Pierino.

Fascination is always directed towards the lively working people of the rural Tuscan village. Elsa's brisk mannerisms at bath time and round-the-clock managerial sturdiness ensure order and protection, while the maid's flashy pink Sunday best attire and gaudy make-up routine are more intriguing to the children than any of the cultured activities scheduled at the Villa. Likewise, the straightforward virulence of their games is a more manageable dynamic for Penny, who is more at ease with the open raucousness and physical exertion required for running and jumping, than the polite and ladylike education she feels she is being chastised with at home. Indeed, for her purported misbehaviour she must wear a dunce hat that calls her bad, lazy and a liar in French – a refinement which does nothing to lessen her shame. Marie shouts when Penny inadvertently breaks her porcelain desk lamp: she does not want her around, she is bad and she is ugly. It is no wonder that Penny chooses to hide in the medlar tree, her skirt falling down over her face as she performs her *gettata* upside down, instead of hurrying inside to join her aunt and cousins for tea.

Penny is not only an outsider to her extended family, but also an exceptional figure within the Italian literary landscape, where there is a noticeable scarcity of mischievous girl characters. This is a lack made even more obvious by the popularity of the trope in its masculine iterations. In 1957, Italo Calvino invented the figure of Cosimo Piovasco di Rondò, the noble-born boy at the heart of *The Baron in the Trees* (*Il barone rampante*) who refuses to eat his snail soup, quarrels with his father and climbs up a nearby tree. Out of a tantrum comes a major disruption to the late eighteenth-century status quo, as Cosimo opts out of life on the ground in order to live among the branches. Elsewhere, Carlo Collodi's wooden Pinocchio laughs at his maker Geppetto as soon as he has finished carving him a mouth, while journalist and satirist Luigi Bertelli's bratty schoolboy Gian Burrasca describes his manifold pranks and tricks – which gain him his "tempestuous" nickname – and the inefficacy of the disciplinary actions with which the adults in his life attempt to regulate his boisterousness. Mazzetti's Penny resembles these characters – and many more like them – and yet is a lone figure. Her gender strips her unruliness of the endearing comic qualities granted to the boys: her impatience with authority sours into self-loathing, her sprightliness fades into malice, her flights of fancy are unnerving rather than dazzling. Calvino's Cosimo attempts to blow up the order he despises, yet Mazzetti's Penny seems unable to contest the structure of her world beyond the occasional stunt. She shares Pinocchio's amazement at the reality she lives in, but her sheltered environment inhibits the development of the empathy that would make her into a real person. Even her farcical suicide attempt is presented as endearingly rash; the realisation of the emotional harm she causes to her uncle never quite arrives. Devoid of comic edges, mischief is just disturbance, and the capricious child whose innermost longing is for adult approval will probably grow up to become a paranoid people-pleaser rather than a self-sufficient individual.

What Penny realises, once the sky has shattered over her head, is her utter powerlessness: "What can a child do to change the rules or the choices of grownups? Nothing." Mazzetti will later say in a 2019 interview with Massimiliano Scuriatti (*Una vita, mille vite*). There is no growth for Penny, no absorption into civil society, no peace-making with her elders and peers: Mazzetti has Penny growing increasingly sad and angry, and her teenage years – which she chronicles in the subsequent episodes of her autobiographical trilogy – eventually turn her into a full-blown anarchist, albeit a suicidal and anti-social one. Teenage Penny is blinded by her grief and unable to translate it into political action. Instead, she searches for a gun, fantasising about shooting somebody with it or of setting off an explosive bomb. In the end, what the teenage-era books amount to are pages filled with notes about squandered days. Yet the meandering, unsettled quality that characterises Mazzetti's later novels does not amount to a kind of failure: rather, it stresses how confrontation, understanding and closure remain unachievable for Penny.

The poet and critic Cristina Campo – herself almost equal in age to Mazzetti – wrote in one of the longest among her many poetic essays, 'Il flauto e il tappeto' ('The Flute and the Carpet,' 1971), that in fairy tales the hero must learn to lose, accept and become one with their loss. Conventional fairy and children's tales might retain and foster their protagonist's potentiality for choice – either to side with conventionality, linger in its vicinity, or reject it altogether – but Penny watches the social order explode and feels the ground crumbling beneath her feet. The slaughter of her adoptive family finally wipes out any semblance of a fable from the story of her childhood and the crushing it entails will soon extend to every corner of her reality.

"The pathway of a fairy tale starts with no earthly hope," writes Campo in the essay chapter 'Della fiaba' ('On fairy tales'), before using the image of a peach and its pit to describe the situation that the fairy-tale hero must face. Just like a peach whose pit breaks away from its pulp, the hero must surrender to a separation between heart and body in order to accomplish the task ahead. They must inhabit a different logic and "read an overworld in its filigree". Crucially, they are asked to belong to and "to sleepwalk" across two worlds at the same time. *The Sky is Falling* gives us – its non-heroic readers – an insight into the soul-splitting process Campo describes. We witness, in the book's finale, a body that goes on living after its heart has received a near-fatal blow. This is the end of the fairy tale: Penny's splitting is unwilled. Extreme violence causes an imperfect metamorphosis. What Campo envisages for the hero, a "tender re-education of one soul's attention", is here sidetracked, sabotaged, and traumatised. The monster lives on and the last scene of the novel sees Penny and Baby hallucinate an English-speaking Don Quixote at the cemetery. The knight offers the sisters sweets before heading back to the woods or – as Penny suggests – towards the windmills. Any hope of closure, let alone salvation, disintegrates.

Mazzetti continuously revisits and inhabits this liminal stuckness throughout her work. Not only will Penny remain detached well into her late adolescence, as the subsequent novels show, but Mazzetti's films *K* (1954) and *Together* (1956) display similar iterations of this kind of lonely survival. The Kafka-inspired protagonist of *K* lives with the burden of a delusional carapace – the original insect-body transformation is twisted into a case of deep depression – that alienates him from everyone around him. The deaf-mute friends in *Together* drift aimlessly across a war-torn cityscape, unable to communicate even when doing so would save their lives. Giving into defeat, however, is not an admission of subservience to the status quo and nor is it self-abnegation. Mazzetti's characters are wanderers, beings at odds with the cold logics of their social worlds, but they live *with,* rather than *through,* their frailty, pain and inadequacy. To endure the forwards thrust of life they cling to the tiniest footholds available with a quiet resolution. The attention they devote to seeing things – *every* thing – come into being allows them to manage unendurable demands and ultimately to keep on living. They look down at the shards of broken skies and up again at the new chalky shapes taking shape overhead. Sleepwalking between these worlds will not do; Mazzetti's losing heroes need more than their own hearts to slice open. And so they must continue to gaze into the blankness despite its blinding glare.

Works cited

Bertelli, Luigi. *Il giornalino di Gian Burrasca*. Giunti, 1990.

Calvino, Italo. *Il barone rampante*. Mondadori, 1993.

Campo, Cristina. *Gli imperdonabili*. Adelphi, 1987.

Collodi, Carlo. *Pinocchio*. Rizzoli, 1991.

Ditlevsen, Tove. *Childhood, Youth, Dependency. The Copenhagen Trilogy*. Penguin, 2021.

Ernaux, Annie. Écrire la vie. Gallimard, 2020.

Ginzburg, Natalia. *Lessico famigliare*. Einaudi, 1972.

Mazzetti, Lorenza. *Con rabbia*. La nave di Teseo, 2016.

— *Diario londinese*. Sellerio, 2014.

— *Il cielo cade*. Sellerio, 2018.

— *Mi può prestare la sua pistola per favore?* La nave di Teseo, 2016.

Scuriatti, Massimiliano. *Una vita, mille vite: conversazione con Lorenza Mazzetti*. La nave di Teseo, 2021

34

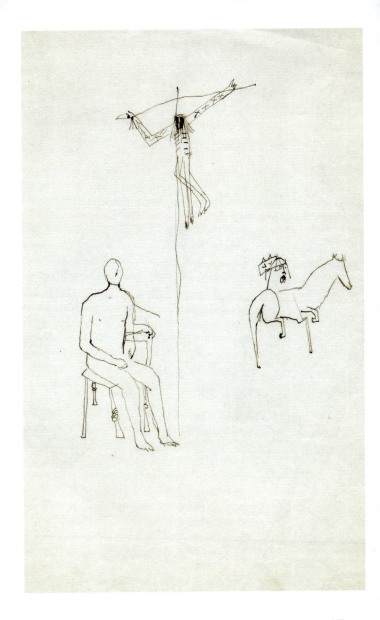

41

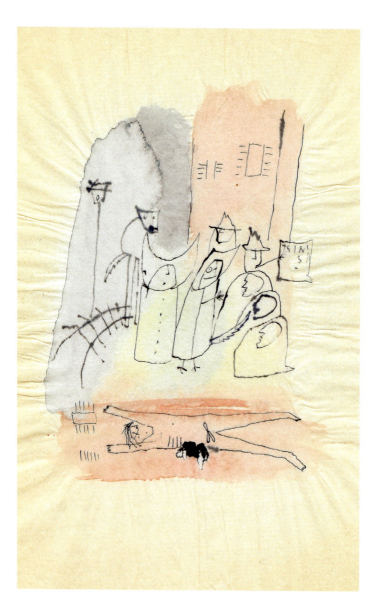

44

The Sky is Falling

Lorenza Mazzetti

(1)

[EXERCISE:] WHAT DID YOU DO AT SCHOOL TODAY?
[ANSWER:] *At school today the Duce told us we should exercise regularly so that we can become strong, resilient and ready to be called upon to defend our great country of Italy because there is a war.*

I wonder if I am allowed to love my sister Baby more than I love the Duce. The trouble is that I love Baby like I love Jesus. Just like I love Jesus. And I love Jesus a little more than God, and God as much as I love Mussolini, and Italy and the Fatherland a little less than God but still more than my yellow bear.

After handing in my writing journal, I looked at the photograph of the Duce stuck on the front cover of my mathematics workbook. On the back of the book there was a picture of the King, His Majesty Vittorio Emanuele the Third, King of Italy. I stared at the Duce intently. I stared him straight in the eye to make sure I was right. Yes, the Duce was good.

The Duce appeared in several guises: from the front, from the side, sometimes with a helmet on his head, and at other times with a laurel wreath like an ancient Roman. On the cover of my workbook, the Duce appeared shirtless among the peasants, harvesting wheat. On the cover of another, he was surrounded by many children in their Figli della Lupa uniforms, and a group of *Piccole Italiane* wearing dresses just like mine. His gaze was kind and intense, just like Jesus's gaze in the picture of him among the children that was printed inside my book of religion.

The Duce also hung above our teacher's head and below him was a crucifix. Then there was a picture of the Duce and the Fürher in profile, smiling at one another. The Fürher was the governor of Germany, and he was great friends with the Duce. I, too, would have liked to be friends with the Duce.

The girl who sat next to me smelled of cheese. My little sister Baby was in another class. She didn't smell like cheese or sheep. Everyone called me Penny, and I didn't smell like cheese either, although whenever I played with Pasquetta, Pierino, Zeffirino and Lea, I ended up smelling like a barn. Pasquetta – the girl who sat next to me – often smelled like salami, especially when she had been eating her mother's sandwiches, but she also had a permanent smell that was uniquely her own. All of the children smelled like hay and sheep.

Our teacher gave us homework for the following day. We were to write an essay on the dream we'd had the night before.

WHAT DID YOU DREAM ABOUT LAST NIGHT?

'What did you dream about last night, Penny?' Lea asked me the next day.

'Leave me alone, goose.'

Lea began to snigger because she'd read something funny in my journal. I wasn't sure what.

My name was foreign and it sounded strange among so many others like Pierino, Pierino the first, Pierino the second. With my starched white smock, shiny shoes, clean legs, neck and ears, I often felt ashamed in the midst of so many children that smelled like haystacks. Lea stood up.

Lorenza Mazzetti

'Miss! Penny dreamt the Madonna had no hair!'

'That the Madonna had no hair? What are you saying...! Be quiet and sit down.'

Lea stopped laughing.

'The Madonna is not bald!' said the teacher. She made me bring her my exercise book and scratched an ugly red mark across the page. Her face was red too.

I burst into tears. The teacher scared me because she was always so hot and bothered and looked at me with such a serious face.

'But I dreamt it!'

'Be quiet!'

'It's true! It's true! I dreamt it!'

She slapped me hard, twice, and sent me off to the corner to stand facing the wall. Later, she reported what had happened to the priest.

'The Devil is in this little girl's house,' the priest said, 'and we must help her. We must make every effort to ensure that she and her family do not go to Hell. Penny can be saved, but her uncle? He is condemned to eternal suffering.'

'And you, Penny? Do you believe in God?'

'I do!'

'But your family... And your uncle...' he bent over me, 'He doesn't believe. He never sends you to Mass. He who does not believe in God is in Satan's hands.'

Thinking about it, I had to agree that Uncle looked a little like he had the Devil inside him, especially when he scolded me.

'We must save them, we must save these two creatures and their family.'

The priest said that Uncle's soul was in danger because he was a Jew, which meant he didn't believe in Jesus, and that the Jewish people had killed Jesus. In order to save him we would have to perform "good deeds". Every little sacrifice, no matter how small, had value. With many sacrifices and renunciations, it might at least be possible to win a place in purgatory for Uncle, who would otherwise be condemned to the eternal fires of Hell. After this the priest dwelt on all the different types of pain people endured in Hell. There were so many that I wondered how the damned didn't die from their punishments.

'Is it true that they walk on dried beans with cut feet?' Zeffirino asked.

After Hell, the priest went on to talk about all the different types of torture that existed in our world.

The bell rang, marking the end of the school day, and we sang *Giovinezza*, and then *Il Piave*. The teacher didn't like it when we shouted the songs and when we ended the anthems with *boom boom*! So we shouted: 'The Piave river murmured: No foreigner shall pass! *Boom boom*!'

I wondered why the Duce's head was so bald and beautifully polished, but I preferred not to ask the teacher about it because of the bald Madonna in my dream, who – now that I thought about it – looked just like the Duce.

The Duce even had a halo around his head, just like a saint.

My favourite song in the world was the song of the Piccole Italiane:

We are the golden dawn,
Growing up gaily in the air and sun,
Of our great Italy we are the girls,
Desiring to make Italy greater forever more.

Our hearts are tiny,
Tiny but ardent with love,
As the warbling fiches singing in chorus,
Iddio pregan: salva il Duce ognor.

(2)

Once lessons were over for the day, Baby and I would be left with the custodian at the school gates, where we would wait for the car that would take us back up to the Villa. There weren't many cars around in those days and ours was a De Soto that came with a chauffeur, so everyone would stare. The chauffeur bundled us into the car, shut the doors and started the engine. All the other boys and girls couldn't help but wave as the car set off. They watched as it ascended the country lane before disappearing into the steep mountain. The people we passed would move out of the way, taking off their hats in reverence.

Baby and I hadn't been living at the Villa for very long. The De Soto was a big car all covered in velvet inside. Uncle Wilhelm's chauffeur wore golden buttons and had sideburns; his name was Cosimo, and at the Villa he also doubled up as a butler.

Cosimo intimidated me and Baby nearly as much as Uncle did. Baby and I had never met Uncle before we'd come to live with him. Papà had told us about him, but now Papà was gone and so was Mamma. They were in the sky. From up there, they looked down on Baby and me to check if we were behaving and if we were being as good, disciplined and respectful as they wished us to be. They had gone up there specifically to keep an eye on us.

THE SKY IS FALLING   51

The chauffeur would often say that Baby and I were two poor orphans and that he pitied us, though I wasn't sure why. But I did really like it when people called me 'poor girl' and patted my head.

The trouble was that since Papà and Mamma had disappeared up to the sky nobody came to give us a hug before bed or in the morning when we woke up, and it would be this way until they came back down to earth. And I wasn't quite clear on when exactly that was meant to happen.

Uncle Wilhelm's estate was very large, so large that it would take him up to a year to survey it all on horseback. Every day he would ride out to see the peasants and ask them, 'How are we doing? How is the sainfoin coming along?' The peasants would take off their hats and respond, 'Our respects!'

When Baby and I had arrived here for the first time, we had curtsied for Aunt Katchen, our father's sister, who'd given us a big hug, and for our cousin Marie too. Annie, on the other hand, had been jealous of our arrival, or so Elsa, the cook, had told us. She had been afraid that Uncle and Aunt would love us more than her, their own daughter.

That was why, that first day, as soon as we had gone into the garden to play with the rocking horse and the other toys, Annie had told us that we weren't allowed to because all the toys were hers. Baby and I had pulled on her plaits, but only because she'd already been kicking and shoving us. Annie had started screaming so loudly that Uncle had come. He'd said, 'Penny, you bad girl! Why are you pulling on Annie's plaits?' Annie had kept on crying, and Uncle had punished us because it wasn't fair of us to gang up on her, two against one. He'd spoken to us about 'Justice'.

Lorenza Mazzetti

I'd cried a lot and then I'd gone to stand between Elsa's knees so she would comfort me, and Baby had followed. Elsa always smelled like onion and wore a chain around her neck with a cross that dangled between her breasts whenever she leaned over to cuddle me. I often felt as if there were a warm tunnel there where I would have liked to have hidden myself away while she sang *Ave Maria*, her voice rising up to the sky.

Elsa bathed us, brushed our hair, and dressed us in our white school smocks and big starched blue bows that smelled like clean laundry. But Elsa really got on my nerves whenever she insisted on washing my neck, my nose, and my ears. Baby would start screaming. I thought that at my age I was old enough to wash myself but Elsa was always convinced that my neck was dirty. So I would say, 'Where is it dirty, Elsa? Where? Show me!'

Then we would climb into the big car again and the chauffeur would take us down the steep road to the village school, which was named Rosa Maltoni after the Duce's mother.

The teacher had given us a warm welcome when we'd first arrived. Then she'd said that all the other children had to treat us kindly, because Baby and I hadn't a mother or a father.

(3)

Uncle was playing chess with Aunt Katchen. Aunt Katchen was a Protestant and so were Marie and Annie. They all believed in God and Jesus but they didn't go to church because Uncle wouldn't allow it, and this was because he wasn't a Christian but a Jew, so he didn't believe in Jesus.

Whenever they played chess, Uncle and Aunty would sit facing one another for hours, looking deadly serious. That was the reason I was terrified of Uncle: he always looked so serious and often scared me when he was angry. He could go whole days without speaking to me. My biggest joy was when Uncle deigned to play chess with me.

Elsa was scrubbing our hands, saying, 'What do you two do with ink? Drink it?'

At the dinner table, Uncle spoke at length about business, or so I imagined because all the grown-ups were speaking German. That night, Uncle's cousin Maya and her husband Pit were over for dinner, as well as Edith, who was Uncle's sister, Arthur, her husband, and their Pekingese dog. Aunt Katchen was teaching us French and English and so we referred to her simply as 'Aunty'. Whenever she spoke to us, she would do so in one or the other, which was annoying because we were expected to respond in the same language when all I wanted to do was to go and sit on the rocking chair. Annie always made it to the chair before me. Throughout dinner, all three of us would be wriggling in our seats until Uncle finally said we were free to go. Then we'd all jump up and race over to the rocking chair. In doing so, we'd often smash a plate or two.

Marie asked me why my eyes were red. I told her that my eyes were red because I'd had a dream about the bald Madonna. I was very upset when Uncle and everyone else, even Aunty, burst out laughing. Everyone was laughing and looking at me and saying,

'The bald Madonna!' Then they'd all start laughing again. Aunty kept repeating the sentence in French and then in German, and somebody had to slap her hard on her back because she couldn't stop laughing and looked like she was about to choke.

I was becoming more and more sure that the Devil was in the Villa. We needed to save everyone. Marie and Annie and the others too.

Marie was studying violin and so was Annie.

I loved Marie but I didn't like Annie as much because she was always playing tricks on me and Baby. Even so, I didn't think she deserved to go to Hell. Depending on her mood, Annie would play with me and Baby or she'd put on Marie's heels and pretend to belong to the world of the grown-ups. Despite this, she was still possessive of her toys and wouldn't let us touch them. Annie was also extraordinarily strong, so there was nothing Baby and I could do to resist her when she came for our pinecones.

Marie was good. Her schoolmates often came round to play tennis with her. Out of all of them, I liked Leonardo the best. I liked him because he sometimes played ping pong with me. I often went out to pick flowers for Marie to arrange in the drawing room and in the guest bedrooms. Marie was good: I didn't want her to go to Hell. But she didn't know that and was cross with me that evening because I had broken the porcelain lamp on her desk.

'Go away, you bad girl!' she'd shouted at me, crouching down to pick up the pieces.

'But I didn't do it on purpose.'

'You and Baby are always breaking things!'

'Don't say that.'

I had started to pick up the pieces of porcelain.

They had been eighteenth-century ladies dancing a minuet around Marie's lamp.

'Bad girl!' Marie had kept on saying.

'Everybody in this house is always telling me off! Nobody knows how much I love you,' I'd told her, walking towards the door. 'If I were a man, I would marry you.'

Only Jesus and the Madonna knew that my heart was not bad. But if God knew everything, perhaps he also knew who was there before Him...

Mister Pit was teaching Annie and Marie how to play the violin. Marie was the better player – she could already do Corelli – whereas Annie was always out of tune and had only just about managed to learn *Oh Tannenbaum* and *Stille Nacht* in time for Christmas.

That evening Mister Pit asked Aunt Katchen to dance. He lifted Aunty onto her feet and started dancing with her, twirling her from left to right like a doll, while his wife Maya played the piano. Maya often sneaked us sweets from Mister Pit's hoard, each time giving us a little kiss on the cheek.

Though he was very rich, Mister Pit dressed badly, using a piece of rope to hold up his trousers instead of a belt. He often forgot to button them up altogether. Aunt Katchen said he never washed, but according to Uncle, Mister Pit was an eccentric genius who played the piano like nobody else. Mister Pit had a passion for our Angora cat, Giovanni, and took long walks with him, talking to him at length. We would spy on Mister Pit and listen to his speeches. He was short-sighted and couldn't see very well and so we would hide in the bushes and go 'Meooow! Meooow!', pretending to be the cat.

As well as playing the piano and whistling while doing so, as if he were also the violin, Mister Pit was a keen mountain climber. He would set off on his walks early in the morning, dressed as if he were about to scale a cliff. Once we discovered a lot of sweets in his room. Nasty man! He never gave us any! I got my own back by playing tricks on him. For instance, I'd put all the sweets in my mouth before wrapping them up again and placing them back on his bedside table. Mister Pit also played chess with Uncle, and whenever he lost he would shut himself away in the bedroom, refusing to come down for breakfast or dinner. Uncle would send dinner up to his room but Mister Pit always refused to open the door and ate his sweets instead.

One evening as we all sat in the drawing room listening to a concert on the radio, Mister Pit rushed down the stairs and barged into the room with a red face, so angry that his eyes looked as if they were about to pop out of his head.

'*Genug! Genug!*' he shouted to everyone's surprise. He threw himself at the radio and turned it off, pummelling it with his fists.

But Mister Pit!

'This be very bad!' And he sat down at the piano to play the same piece himself. Everyone was silent. Mister Pit was Uncle's friend so he could do whatever he wanted, and even come down to dinner without washing his hands. I was jealous of him.

Mister Pit played and played. His hands flew across the keys. Everyone listened admiringly.

He stopped for a moment and ripped his starched collar and tie off his neck, tossing them to the floor. Then he resumed playing. The house was full of notes. Mister Pit was hitting the piano with his quick fingers as if he were taking something out on it. He stopped again to throw his jacket to the floor and then resumed his furious playing, biting down on his lip and making hideous faces. Everyone was in raptures. But I was waiting for him to take off his cuffs and waistcoat. A moment later his cuffs flew over our heads and hit Mister Arthur, who raised his hands to shield himself.

After a few more frenzied chords, Mister Pit concluded his concert and stood up.

'*Wunderbar*!' Uncle said. The others clapped while Baby and I went to gather Mister Pit's scattered clothes in order to return them to him.

(4)

Our cook, Elsa, our chauffeur, Cosimo, and our maid, Rosa, went to Mass every Sunday. There was a private chapel on the grounds of the Villa and the priest came there to officiate. All the peasants went along for the service, but Uncle didn't, and he didn't let us go either.

Rosa was in love with Nello, one of the peasants, and Pierino's mother said that Nello had made her a baby from too much kissing. On Sundays Rosa smelled lovely, though on every other day she smelled like onions. She would stand in front of the mirror to get ready while Baby and I looked on.

'Good Lord, I'm so fat!' she'd say.

Uncle didn't want us spending time with Rosa and the peasant children because then we'd forget how to speak proper Italian. Baby and I spent time with them anyway, in secret. Rosa had a shocking pink dress and once she'd covered her face with so much powder that she no longer looked like herself, she would leave. And then she would rush back to the mirror again to check that all was in order. After half an hour of looking at herself, her eyes would glaze over.

'Rosa, why do you keep looking at yourself?'

She would shush me, but she also always took my advice. I would take the comb and run it through her hair, and so would Baby, and then we would curl it to make her look beautiful.

'Sweet mother Mary, is this dress too tight?' she asked me, 'Should I pin this rose to my chest, Penny?'

'Further up!' Rosa moved it up an inch.

'Further down!' Rosa moved it back down again. Her eyes fell to her belly.

'Men. Pigs,' she said.

'What's that?'

'Pigs. All of them. Including Mussolini.' She left, slamming the door.

I loved Rosa, but I couldn't stand her talking about the Duce in that way. I knew it was Nello who put ideas like this in her head. I'd have to kill Rosa if I heard her say bad things about Benito Mussolini again.

Back then, Baby and I lived in the trees with the peasant children: Lea, Pasquetta, Zeffirino, Pierino. There was a thick wood of old laurels behind the Villa. We spent most of our time there playing *la gettata*.

La gettata was a game that involved jumping from one branch to the next, followed by a *capucertola*, a special backflip that was performed by somersaulting to a third branch and hanging upside down from it by only the backs of your knees.

One time Baby fell and hurt her back. How scary! She cried loads.

'Does it hurt, Baby? You can have all my pinecones if you stop crying.'

Pasquetta brought her some cold water and we made her compresses of wet sand and leaves.

Leonardo came every day. He lived on a nearby mountain. He would visit on horseback. One day I asked him if he knew how to climb trees, but he said no. So I took him to the laurel woods and said that I would show him how to play *la gettata*. I indulged myself by showing off all my best backflips, holding onto the branches by my knees with my head hanging down. I even showed him *l'angelo*, dangling off a branch with my arms spread open like wings. Leonardo gave it a try.

'What are you doing up there?' asked Marie, who'd been looking for him. 'Come in for tea.'

Leonardo went up to the Villa and I stayed in my tree, thinking about how much I loved him.

Sometimes when Leonardo came I didn't want to be seen because I had been a bad girl and as punishment I'd been made to wear a paper strip around my head that said: *méchante* or *paresseuse* or *menteuse*. If I didn't practice my French or my English, Aunty made me wear the *chapeau d'âne* and I was so ashamed of it that I would stay tucked away in my medlar tree.

(5)

I had to save Uncle Wilhem, Aunt Katchen, Marie, and Annie, along with the guests and their Pekingese dog. And then, of course, I had to save myself and Baby.

Baby didn't know that the Devil was in our house. Somebody needed to tell her. What if the Devil was also in Baby? I turned around suddenly and thought I glimpsed the Devil in Baby's eyes. I had to tell her.

Baby was under the great oak tree, crouching down to chase a cicada.

'Look, Penny! A dragonfly!'

'It's a cicada!'

Baby leaned forward to take a closer look at the cicada. I leaned forward to take a closer look at Baby. What if the Devil was also in Baby? I tried turning around quickly again, and just like before I thought I saw something evil in Baby's eyes. I told her so. We stood up, turned our backs to one another and began to count, 'One! Two! Three!' We turned around as fast as we could to look into each other's eyes. Baby was staring at me glassy-eyed, without blinking. I became frightened and started to scream, 'Baby! Baby! Answer me!'

But Baby continued to give me the same icy look.

'Baby!' I shouted, shaking her as hard as I could. Baby remained inert, letting me shake her, her gaze fixed on infinity. I tried to make her laugh, but Baby was staring at me with the Devil's eyes. I was so frightened that I began to cry. Baby was right there in front of me with the Devil inside her.

'You're the Devil! You're the Devil!'

Now Baby was jumping around, smiling widely to reassure me. 'Penny, I swear, I'm not the Devil!'

'Are you sure you're not the Devil?'

'Penny, I swear I'm not the Devil. What about you? Are you?' asked Baby, looking into my eyes.

I told Baby the priest had said that the Devil had possessed Uncle and that in order to save him we had to perform "good deeds". The priest had said that there was value in renouncing things, even the smallest thing, and that by renouncing things and making sacrifices we might be able to stop Uncle from going to Hell. The priest had said that there was real fire in Hell, that it really burned, and that it was forever.

'The fire never goes out?'

'Never.'

'What does that mean, never?'

'Never means always. The priest says that not only is there eternal fire in Hell but many other types of suffering. Some devils make the damned walk barefoot on dried beans after they've cut open the soles of their feet.'

I remembered the priest's words perfectly, down to the last detail. He'd described the water drop torture. He'd said that another way to kill people involved rubbing their feet with salt and then sending goats to lick their toes until they died from the tickling.

Later, as we ate, Baby asked Uncle if it was really possible to die from tickling. Uncle said yes and told us about a famous writer called Aretino who'd actually died from laughing too much.

After lunch we went out to the garden.

'How will Uncle die?' Baby asked.

'I don't know. Uncle won't die.'

'No,' said Baby, 'He won't go to Hell. I'll go there in his place.'

'That's not possible.'

'Then you go.'

'It's not possible because of the Last Judgement.'

Baby looked dejected.

'What about if we do good deeds and make sacrifices? Will he still go to Hell then?'

'No.'

'So Uncle won't die in the eternal fire?'

'No, he won't die.'

(6)

'What penance shall we make?'

'Let's try and stand on one foot for as long as we can.'

'That's not a penance. We have to suffer.'

'What should we do to suffer?'

'We must do as the little martyrs do.'

'Let's cross this field of thorns back and forth until our flesh bleeds!'

Lea, Pierino and Zeffirino looked at the spiky field, which was the name we had given the field of dry yellow flowers that had thorns instead of leaves.

I threw myself into the spikes, but I had to stop running halfway across the field because of the pain. The others hadn't moved yet.

'Come on!' I shouted, and I started running again with tears of pain rolling down my cheeks. I was jumping from foot to foot to try and feel it less. I stopped when I reached the other side of the field,

THE SKY IS FALLING   63

writing in agony. The others had only made it to the middle of the spiky field. They stood still, lacking the courage to move either forwards or backwards. There were also nettles hidden among the spikes. I looked down at my legs. They were red and burning. The others were getting closer, jumping and screaming.

Finally they arrived, one after the other.

'Ouch, ouch,' they rolled around on the ground.

Baby was last.

I looked at her legs. They were red too, with lots of tiny thorns still stuck in them. Pasquetta had hitched her dress right up above her thighs and was showing us her legs, 'Look at this!'

Lea squirmed.

'Stop it! Stop it!' She smoothed damp leaves over her thighs and calves in order to soothe the pain.

'No, that's not enough. We said we would run through the field ten times and we've only done it once.'

I started running again and the others followed me. The thorns pierced our legs. We'd all start running shouting *Go!*, screaming like savages to fire ourselves up. The real pain only started later, because of the nettles.

At sundown Uncle appeared at the top of the hill, followed by his guests. He shouted, 'It's late! Penny, Baby, come home!' He waved his hand before continuing with the others in the direction of the Villa. His head was white all over. I felt that I loved him. I looked at my legs, all dotted in red, and wiped Baby's legs with more laurel leaves. Baby was crying, so I picked some berries from the strawberry tree and gave them to her to make her stop.

'I didn't make it to the other side,' Baby said.

She had only made it halfway before she got stuck, unable to move in either direction.

'You're only little though.'

It was getting dark and Zeffirino said, 'I gotta get home or Pa will beat me.' We could hear Zeffirino's father call, 'Zeffirinoooo! You better come home right away, or I'll fix you, I'll fix you alright! You bum! You better go fetch the water!'

When he was angry, Zeffirino's father took off his belt and ran after his son screaming and whipping him with it. Lea and Pierino's mother also slapped them when they didn't do their chores, and if for some reason she couldn't catch them, she'd take off her clogs and throw them after her children.

Oh! How I wished Uncle would whip me with his belt or slap me instead of looking at me with such disdain, not speaking to me or smiling in my direction for days on end!

The maids called us for our bath and then dinner. After dinner, they sent us to bed.

Annie was allowed to stay up ten minutes longer than us because she was older, and so she would sit on the rocking chair like a queen, looking down on us pityingly. We'd kiss Uncle, Aunt Katchen, and Marie on the cheek. We'd curtsy for the guests.

Often, if I had been a bad girl, when I went to kiss Uncle goodnight he would turn his face away and reject me with an air of reproach.

That evening, Annie was sitting on the rocking chair and she tripped me up when I walked past. At once, I leapt at her, half out of envy and half out of rage, going straight for her plaits. When Uncle saw this, he made me fill ten pages in my punishment journal with the sentence: *I must not pull on Annie's plaits.*

In my bedroom, I flipped through the journal. There were hardly any pages left. It was full of sentences like: *I will not lie. I will not throw cups or glasses at people's heads. I will not cut up clothes I don't like. I will be kind, disciplined and respectful. I will not answer back when I am being told off. I will not talk with my mouth full. I will not spy on people through keyholes. I will not trip up the maid. I will not crush the wheat in the field. I will not sully the walls with drawings or with my dirty hands. I will not throw stones at the window. I will not live in the trees. I will not speak too loudly. I will not sing fascist hymns while Uncle sleeps. I will not play with peasants children. I will not fraternise with the servants. I will not go to bed in the clothes I have been wearing all day.*

(7)

The grown-ups were playing cricket. We could hear them laughing. Aunty was sitting on the deckchair in the shade of the mulberry tree, reading *Vol de nuit*.

Uncle had his gold-handled cane by his side. Edith was painting a tree, and her husband Arthur was smoking his pipe next to her. They lived in a nearby villa and held us little ones in much lower regard than they did their Pekingese, dog Cipì, who was treated like a king and bit me every time I came too close to him.

The last of the guests was a big and burly old man with glasses and a ginger moustache whose name was Van Marlen and who dealt with the history of art. He lived on the other side of the mountain and spent long hours with Uncle in his studio stuffed with books.

Whenever Mister Van Marlen arrived in his car, he would stop at the bottom of the stone steps that led to the Villa and stay for a moment to play hopscotch with us. We played this by using a piece of chalk to trace some marks on the ground, which we'd then jump across on one foot. Mister Van Marlen always tried but never won. He was so big and burly that he always fell on the other foot, making Baby laugh and shriek with delight.

Cosimo, the butler, came to tell Mister Van Marlen that tea was ready, and took him away to my and Baby's great outrage. Annie followed him into the drawing room, though not without turning around to make faces at us before she left.

Edith, who was painting the tree, didn't like it when we watched her paint. Of course, this only made us want to watch more, and so we would perch in the highest branches of a nearby tree, silent as mice in our uncomfortable positions for the whole time she was working, just so we could see how a tree was made.

We knew exactly when she would come with her easel and her Pekingese dog, and we'd be waiting for her. I would watch the sky through the tangle of branches, following the various calls of the birds. Lea was even able to imitate them!

'I need to pee,' said Baby that day, her eyes wide. 'Hold it in!'

'Birdbrain needs to pee,' Pasquetta was laughing so much that her branch started to creak.

From our outpost we could see Edith, the painting and the landscape she kept on erasing.

'I can't hold it anymore!' said Baby and she peed.

After that Mrs. Edith was mortally offended and never spoke to us again.

'I feel so much better. I thought I was going to burst!'

'Idiot!'

'You're an idiot!'

'Mouseface!'

'You're a mouseface!' said Baby, climbing down from the tree. She ran away, crying. I was upset.

'Just let her be!' Pasquetta shouted when I called after Baby.

'No, no...' I jumped down from the tree and started running. I could accept anything from life except losing Baby's smiles. If Baby was angry with me, the sky went dark and the sun went black and my heart slowly froze over.

'Baby! Baby!' I shouted, chasing her across the fields. 'Come here! Give me a kiss! Just one!'

But Baby kept running in the grass.

'No!' she said.

'Just one kiss, Baby!'

Finally, she stopped, out of breath.

'Fine,' she planted a tiny wet kiss on my cheek.

Then we hugged and rolled down the green slope with our arms around one another. The others arrived and joined in, rolling through the green sainfoin in pairs. I squeezed Baby as hard as I could and I thought about the fact that my name was Penny and Baby's Baby, and not Penny. But why was I Penny and not Baby? What would I be like if I were Baby?'

'Baby, don't you think it's strange you're not me?'

'What?'

'I love you so much that it seems impossible to me that you're not me. I don't know what you are, and you don't know what I am either.'

'You're Penny.'

'I feel like this tree. What do you feel like?'

Baby said she felt like the grasshopper we could hear singing from somewhere nearby, and I said I felt like that swallow in the sky, and we continued like this for a very long time.

(8)

Let's play doctor and patient.
Who'll be the doctor?

'I will,' said Pierino.

So Lea was the maid and I was Mrs. Smith. Baby was Mister Smith and, as usual, Zeffirino and Pasquetta were the count and countess. Just like that, the doorbell rang. The maid ran to open it.

It was the doctor.

'This is the doctor,' I said, introducing him to the count and countess.

'I'm Mrs. Smith and this is my husband,' I said to the doctor, gesturing towards Baby.

'Would you like something sweet, Mister Doctor?' Pasquetta asked.

'No, thank you, Madame Countess,' said Pierino.

'You're welcome,' said Baby, sticking a cup in the doctor's hand.

'A little tea?' asked Lea.

'Thank you, Mrs. Smith,' said Pierino, taking the cream bun I was offering him and pretending to eat it.

'You are very welcome, Mister Doctor.'

'Do you like cream buns?'

'Of course, Madame Countess, but I like donuts even more.'

'But doctor, you know very well that we only eat donuts on the Festa di San Giuseppe.'

'Another cream bun?' Lea asked Pierino.

'No, thank you.'

'Another cream bun for you, Madame Countess?'

'No, thank you,' said Pasquetta, dabbing the corners of her mouth like a real lady.

'You're making the napkins all red, Countess!' shouted Lea angrily.

'Doesn't matter, I'll wash 'em later,' said the countess.

'What will Uncle say if the stain doesn't come out?' asked Baby with concern.

'Oh! You've got an uncle too?' I said.

'Yes, of course,' said Baby, composing herself, 'I've an uncle and a sister-in-law.'

'I've a sister-in-law myself,' said the countess.

'Is your sister-in-law's cousin better now, Madame Countess?' Pierino asked.

'Yes, thank you, Doctor. It's the father of the bride who is unwell these days.'

'Another cream bun, Mister Doctor?'

'Thank you, but I've already had one.'

'Have another,' said the maid.

'No, thank you, I never eat after eating.'

'But it's the afternoon now.'

'Thanks, but when it's this cloudy it already feels as if dinner has long since ended.'

'Awful weather outside,' said Baby, looking at the bright blue sky.

'You're right, the weather is terrible today, Mister Smith,' said Pasquetta, turning up the collar of Aunt Katchen's fur coat and dabbing at her face with her napkin again, which was sweaty because of the intense heat. Off came more powder and lipstick.

'You're staining all my napkins with lipstick!' the maid cried.

'Shut up, you're the maid!'

'Doctor, I'm not feeling well. Could you give me a check-up?' I said.

'I'm not well either,' said the maid.

'Yes, my wife has been a little under the weather,' Baby added.

'Get undressed,' the doctor ordered me.

'Would you like to take off your coat, Mister Doctor?'

'Yes, thank you.'

'Another cream bun, Mrs. Smith?' Zeffirino asked.

'No, thank you. I'm ill.'

I stretched out on the sofa and Pierino bent over to look at me.

'Open your mouth, Mrs. Smith.'

I opened my mouth like sick people do.

'Say *aaaah*,' he knocked his fist across my back. 'Where does it hurt?'

'Everywhere,' I said plaintively.

'Take all your clothes off.'

'Everything?'

'Everything, everything,' Pierino said.

The doctor leaned over to take a closer look, then turned to the others and said, 'We need to operate now.'

'What's wrong?' asked the countess.

'Appendicitis.'

'Appendicitis!' Zeffirino exclaimed. 'Poor Mrs. Smith!'

'Someone needs to put the ether on her face,' said the doctor.

'I'll take care of that, Mister Doctor!'

'Thank you, Madame Countess.'

'You're welcome.' Pasquetta took a napkin, dipped it in some water, and placed it under my nose.

'Don't move,' said Pierino, 'Or I won't be able to operate.'

'I'll keep her still!' Baby butted in, tying my feet to the sofa with a thin piece of rope.

'Thank you, Mister Smith,' said Pierino.

I struggled against them just like I'd seen sick people struggle.

Pasquetta and Zeffirino tied my arms down with pieces of rope, while Baby handed the doctor his knife and pliers.

The doctor bent over me with the knife. Pasquetta had gagged me to give me the ether and the countess was pressing the wet napkin down on my mouth so hard I almost choked. Meanwhile, the doctor ran his hands all over my body, until suddenly he stopped.

'Here,' he said, and he operated.

I waited for Pierino to finish the operation.

'Any better?' asked the doctor once he had finished.

'Yes, much better.'

'You can get dressed now.'

'My turn!' the countess squealed and took off all her clothes.

'A cream bun?' asked the maid.

'No, thank you, I'm ill.'

'Good morning, Madame, how are we doing today?'

'Badly,' Pasquetta said.

Lorenza Mazzetti

'Where does it hurt?'

'Everywhere,' she said.

'An enema will fix that,' said the doctor.

'Of course, Mister Doctor,' said the countess and assumed the position.

Then it was time for dinner and Elsa called us in to wash our hands before eating.

(9)

'You! What do you want?' the priest shouted at Zeffirino, who was waving his hand in the air.

'Father, I need to go...'

'No, not now.'

The priest continued to speak. He said that Pasquetta and Lea and all the others needed to study the doctrine in order to be ready for their confirmation, and that they should teach it to me and Baby in secret instead of just playing games.

'Consider the great evil that is committed when one gravely offends God, our Lord and Father, who has given us so many good things, and who loves us infinitely and deserves our infinite love and to be served with great faith above all other things... You again? What is it now?'

'I can't hold it in anymore!'

'Then go. But come right back.'

Zeffirino slipped out of the classroom.

'Remember that the Passion of our Lord Jesus Christ was caused by our sin and that because of us he was whipped and beaten until he bled. Remember that the soldiers took away his garments and played dice on his tunic. They brought him before Pontius Pilate and asked, "Should we crucify him or Barabbas?" And what do you think Pontius Pilate replied? Barabbas? No! Pontius Pilate ordered that water be brought and washed his hands. What would you have done in Pilate's place? Would you have crucified Jesus, the child of God? Answer me!'

He pointed his finger at us and waited for someone to reply.

'No!' I said, rising to my feet, my eyes red and stinging with tears.

'No, you say?' said the angry priest, 'Even Peter, one of the Apostles, said to Jesus, "Lord, I shall not betray you!" But then he denied him on the night of his Crucifixion, not once but three times! And thrice the rooster cried.'

'Silence!' the priest shouted at the class, 'Don't be so loud or I'll fix you alright!'

He drew his palms together and told us to repeat after him, 'Oh, most merciful Saviour, I have sinned and sinned greatly against you, and thus I am guilty, so terribly guilty...'

We all repeated in unison.

'...of rebelling against your sacred rule and preferring my whims to you, my Lord and heavenly Father.'

I didn't fully understand the meaning of these words. I looked in vain for my sin and could not find it. I felt ashamed. Finally, I thought of something: I hadn't been paying attention to the priest as he prayed. My thoughts had wandered to the games I played in the fields with Baby and the others, to the cicadas that are green when they are born and which look like little maggots before they leave their burrows. After crawling out, they would sit in the sun and I would watch them, and half an hour later they would turn from green to black and sing when Lea tickled their bellies. Lea didn't know you could die from too much laughing.

We all repeated in unison, 'Here I am, my beloved and good Christ and I am at your feet. I pray with burning fervour that you imprint my heart with feelings of faith and hope and charity, and with the pain of my sins and the promise to never again take your name in vain, while I, full of love and compassion for you, contemplate your five holy wounds.'

Now the priest addressed us directly again, shouting and pointing his finger, 'It is your fault if Christ died on the cross! He died for us! He died to wash away our sins, do you understand that?'

He raised his voice even louder, 'On the Day of Judgement, he will return to us and then we will see who will go to Heaven! Perhaps you think that Hell is a nice place? It isn't. It's full of devils and that's why you have to behave better right now, before it's too late!'

In his fury, he was speaking in Florentine dialect.

'So, even if you have the smallest stain, even this little...' and then he pinched his fingers as if to catch a fleck of dust, 'It's gonna show on Judgement Day!'

(10)

When I entered the dining room, everyone was sitting at the table, waiting for us. Resting in the middle of the tablecloth was a beautiful tray piled with cream-filled krapfen. My mouth immediately began to water.

'Here she is, at last!' Aunty exclaimed.

'What have you done? Why is your face all black? Where's Baby?'

'Oh, she's nearby, in the laurel woods,' I said, sitting down to eat.

'What is she doing?'

'We tied her up to play war.'

Uncle and Aunty jumped to their feet. It was starting to rain.

'We were playing war, so we had to tie her up, and we painted our faces black because we were the Abyssinians. Pierino was the Duce on horseback. Baby wanted to be a war hero, dressed in her Piccola Italiana uniform.'

Aunty said, along with many other exaggerations, that Baby was afraid of thunder and would surely catch some kind of illness – all because of a little cold and rain!

It made me angry to see the entire house in disarray and Uncle so irritated about something so silly. The most annoying thing of all was that I couldn't eat the krapfen because I had to show them where Baby was tied up, even though she was actually very proud of playing the hero in her Piccola Italiana uniform.

Uncle was saying terrible things about me and the others were agreeing with him. They said I was disobedient, spiteful and a liar: a child without a heart. And there I was, getting soaked in the rain just to go and get Baby, and unlike her I would receive neither understanding nor krapfen. I was sent up to my room like a dog.

According to them, I brought shame on the family. It was even worse because they were talking about me as if I couldn't hear them. It was always my fault and never Baby's because Baby was younger.

Uncle was all about Justice. Uncle was Justice personified. Had the whole of Justice gathered itself up inside Uncle? Wasn't Justice a woman?

In my bedroom, alone like a dog while Baby ate krapfen.

Soon Uncle came knocking on my door. He wanted to know if I was sorry. I didn't answer him. I was not sorry because I was not guilty. But Uncle would never have understood that because of his obsession with telling the truth, like a man who had swallowed Lady Justice.

Uncle knocked at the door but I kept quiet. I hid my head under the bedsheets. No, I wasn't bad, no, I wasn't wicked, no, I wasn't ungrateful. I stayed silent. What if Uncle knocked the door down?

'Answer me, Penny.'

I jumped out of my sheets and shouted back, 'No! I won't ask for forgiveness! I'm not bad, I'm not bad, I'm not bad!'

Uncle went away and ordered Marie not to let me out of my room until I had written a hundred lines of: *I will not answer back when I am being told off by a grown-up.*

Grown-ups, grown-ups. Grown-ups were always right and us little ones were powerless: my truth wasn't true but neither were my lies.

But I believed in my lies, and I believed – I firmly believed – that I was good and had never done anything evil, and I wanted to prove to Uncle that I loved him.

Only how could I prove it to him? He had no idea that I would have given my life for him.

THE SKY IS FALLING

Baby said she would give her life for Uncle, too, and even her soul.

Uncle said he'd much prefer it if we were good, obedient and respectful. Oh, how I wished that Uncle would beat me instead of holding a grudge against me for such a long time!

Uncle came back several times, but I stayed locked in my bedroom because I didn't want to say sorry.

In the afternoon, having seen Baby playing in the garden and because I was getting hungry, I suddenly ran down the stairs screaming, 'I'm sorry, I'm sorry! I'm a bad girl!'

Elsa made me one sandwich filled with ham and another filled with cheese, and I went outside to find Baby. When Baby saw me, she gave me a big smile and some of the pinecones she'd been cracking open. It had stopped raining and the snails had come out. For a while, we watched the snails. Then Pierino began to collect them for draining and eating.

To make Uncle happy I made the face of somebody who had been evil but had repented. Uncle said that it wasn't so hard to be good, at least for a few days: all you had to do was begin, and the rest would follow.

(11)

We met every day under the big oak tree to practice our catechism.

'For what purpose did God create us?'

'God created us to know, love and serve him in this life, so that we may take pleasure in his presence in the next life in Heaven.'

'What is Heaven?'

'Heaven is the eternal enjoyment of God, who is our happiness, and through him of every other goodness in the absence of all evil.'

'I don't understand,' Baby whined.

'Baby isn't ever going to get it, she's just wasting our time. For God's sake, she can't stand still for a minute, always looking at ants. Of course you aren't going to understand if you don't listen,' said Pasquetta.

'The flies are pinching me!' said Baby.

'I'll pinch you if you're not careful!'

'Penny, you explain it to Baby. It really is simple. It means that God's in Heaven, and we'll join him there to love and serve him and have a good time. What's so difficult to understand? You tell me.'

'Let's carry on,' said Pierino.

Since I was lying on my stomach on the grass, his feet were level with my face. They smelled like hay.

'Who is allowed into Heaven?'

Lea and Pasquetta replied in unison, 'He who is good, and has loved and served God faithfully and dies in his grace deserves to go to Heaven. He who is bad, who doesn't serve him and dies in mortal sin deserves Hell.'

They finished at the same time.

'But why is Uncle bad?' asked Baby.

'Mister Master is bad because he hasn't been baptised and because he is a Jew,' Zeffirino said.

'The priest said so,' added Lea.

'My uncle is good,' Baby insisted.

'Uncle is good,' I repeated.

'No, the Master hasn't been baptised, and original sin can only be cleansed by holy baptism, so he's a sinner.'

'And what is original sin?' Baby asked, increasingly whiny and resentful.

'Original sin is the sin that mankind committed... committed...' Pasquetta didn't know how to continue. Lea picked up and said in one quick breath, 'That mankind committed through Adam, the first man, and with which every man is tainted as his natural descendants.'

Then she added, 'And since among the sons of Adam only the holy Virgin Mary was spared, we must pray to the Virgin, because she is sinless, pure, so pure... Can't you see what an innocent face she has?'

We looked at the Virgin Mary depicted in the book.

'Such rosy lips! Her eyes look like dew drops!' said Lea.

'There's a snake under her foot!'

'Yes, but it can't hurt her. Can't you see? The Madonna is crushing it with her foot.'

'The snake is the Devil who has come to lead her into temptation.'

'Yes, but Uncle is good, and he will go to Heaven,' said Baby.

'The priest said the Master is foreign and he's gonna go to Hell because Jews don't believe in Jesus or the Virgin Mary.'

'That's not true. Uncle Wilhelm isn't going to go to Hell.'

'No, he will,' said Pasquetta, 'because he never comes to Mass, and he never sends you either, and he doesn't teach you the doctrine. If we weren't teaching you ourselves, you'd be on your way to Hell too.'

'It's true,' said Zeffirino, looking stern.

'But I'm scared!' said Baby, bursting into tears.

Pierino said, 'It's not true, the two of them won't go because they were baptised before their mother died. Even the priest said so.'

'Don't you remember your ma?'

'No,' Baby said.

'And you, Penny? Don't you remember her?'

'No,' I said, straining my memory. My first memory was of Baby. Baby and I on a balcony, swallows in the sky. I remember that the house was in Piazza di Spagna and that the concierge was called Rosina. We were born there. Papà had been working as a company director. We lived there until we were three but all I could remember about it was the balcony, the roofs, the swallows and the sound of cars. The house was empty and all I remembered was Baby. Papà was always out working as a company director and our German nanny would lock us inside after leaving our meals on the table. If we didn't like what she'd made, we'd hide it under the cushions of the armchair. Our German nanny was young and beautiful and her name was Lucy. One time Baby and I had climbed up the green trellis covered in twisting wisteria. We had almost made it to the top when we saw an old man in the window opposite who was gesticulating at us, swinging his head back and forth with a grave expression as if to say 'No'. In order to get a better look, we'd climbed even higher, dangling off the slats and waving enthusiastically. Suddenly, the door below had opened and lots of people had poured out onto our balcony, telling us to climb back down with big smiles on their faces. When we finally had we'd both been very upset to receive such a beating and had begun to cry.

'No one's ever taken you to Mass? Never ever?' Zeffirino asked.

One day my father had come home with a doll that was so big it terrified us, and he'd put us in the car and deposited us with his painter friend Ugo and his wife Renata, who had three girls of their own. Everyone had showered us with hugs and kisses. Renata was the first person to tell us about Jesus.

Renata had put us on the train and dropped us off here, with Papà's sister Katchen and Uncle Wilhelm, because Papà had gone off in his car to join Mamma in the sky.

But Uncle never hugged us, Annie played tricks on us, and Aunty made us sit through those terrible hours of English and German in the shade of the holly oak while the cicadas sang loudly, and Lea and Zeffirino spied on us through the bushes.

Renata had told us, 'Be good and don't make Uncle angry.' And then she'd disappeared.

'They really don't teach you anything at home. Didn't they even tell you about Adam and Eve?'

'No,' Baby replied, 'they didn't tell us about Adam and Eve.'

One day Renata had given us a prayer book in which, it's true, there had been a picture of Adam and Eve, and another of the angel Gabriel, with his burning sword. She'd given it to us before we arrived at the Villa, and she'd told us that Uncle was very rich and so it was better for us to stay there, but that we should always remember her and Jesus, and angel Gabriel, and her beloved infant Saint John.

'Do you at least know how many sins there are?'

'No,' said Baby.

'Original sin, actual sin, mortal sin.'

'Original sin is erased by holy Baptism. Actual sin is that which is voluntarily committed by people of their own free will. Actual sins are of two kinds: venial and mortal.'

We all repeated after him.

'I don't understand,' said Baby.

'Shut up, you!' Zeffirino said, 'The Devil was also good once, but then he went bad, so God cast him down from Heaven.'

He rounded his lips to imitate the Devil and said in a screeching voice, 'Alright then, I'll be headin' down, but you gotta send me some souls!'

'And what did the Madonna say?' Baby asked.

'The Virgin wasn't there yet though, was she? She only came when it was time to give birth to our Lord Jesus Christ, and none of it – the angel coming down with a lily in his hand for Mary and all that – had happened yet.'

'The story goes like this: God created Adam and Eve, and then the Devil came up to the earth to tempt them and said in his screechy voice, "Eat the apple, Eve! Eat the apple, Adam!"'

'Was his voice really so screechy?'

Pasquetta began to imitate the voice of the Devil too.

'Really really?'

'Yes, yes, the priest does it that way. They really don't teach you anything at home. They never tell you about Adam and Eve and the Devil?'

'No.'

'The Devil is in the Villa, the priest said so. And the Master will go to Hell, 'cause he ain't baptised. You can get baptised even as a grown-up, as long as you do it before you die.'

'And how do you do it?'

'With water on your head'

'Why don't we baptise Uncle, then?'

'To begin with, you're not a priest.'

'No, all we can do is pray fervently and offer Masses for him.'

'But Uncle isn't dead!' I shouted.

'No, but we're doing it to save his soul.'

'Yes, but Uncle is so good... Don't you think Jesus will let him into Heaven anyway?'

'No,' said Pasquetta, 'and even if Jesus did allow it, Satan would be right there, ready to grab him and whip him.'

'Whip him?'

'He'll whip him first, and then he'll toss him into the fire with all of the other damned.'

'Real fire?'

'Of course. The priest said so.'

Baby began to cry again.

'How does the priest know all of this?'

'Sorry, Penny, but do you really think you know more than the priest? What do you think priests and bishops are there for? My goodness, this girl...'

'I don't want Uncle to end up in the fire!'

I started sobbing, 'I don't want it! I don't want it!' I leapt at Pasquetta.

'Shut up then! I'm saying that your uncle won't go to Hell if we pray for his soul and make sacrifices.'

'Jews don't have souls.'

'That's why we need to do penitence,' everybody said in unison.

'Yes, penitence,' Lea repeated. 'And the more we suffer, the better.'

(12)

[EXERCISE:] WE LOVE MUSSOLINI AS IF HE WERE OUR OWN FATHER.

[ANSWER:] *I love Benito Mussolini more than my own father because my father is not here. I am always with my uncle, and so I love Mussolini like I love Uncle.*

Then I asked the teacher if I could go to the toilet. Next to the toilet, there was a beautiful bunch of flowers. Each of us had a little jar on our desk to put flowers in. Sometimes the jar toppled over, spilling water all over our workbooks and ruining them. Despite this, our teacher's desire to make a good impression on the local party officer persisted, though we were never quite sure when he might arrive. He could have come at any time. In fact, he might have been making his way up the stairs at that very moment accompanied by his men. When the party officer finally did arrive, he would appear out of the blue, dressed in his fascist uniform. He would be driven to the school along with the other gentlemen. His black car would be covered in mud by the time it reached our school, and one time it had stopped right next to a puddle and the officer had become very angry because he had got his shoes dirty. That day, us girls were all wearing their Piccole Italiane uniforms and the boys were dressed as Figli della Lupa. We were singing in chorus, *Vesta's fire, bursting out of the temple*. The teacher was all flustered and kept reminding us to sing and not yell. We weren't yelling but the party officer raised his hands to his ears as if to tell us that we were making too much of a racket. There was also a woman officer with him, who inspected us to see if we passed muster. She was dressed completely in black with golden insignia on her shoulders.

'You! Come forward!' said the local party officer. I didn't know whether he was speaking to me or Pasquetta and I was too afraid to move. He started shouting, 'You! The potato on the left! Come forward!'

When I heard the word potato, I began to suspect he really was talking about me, so I stepped forward and he told me off for wearing yellow shoes. I had told Marie and Elsa to let me wear black shoes that morning, but Uncle had come into the room and said, 'The yellow ones are fine.'

'Yes,' I'd told Uncle, 'but I'm a Piccola Italiana and I want to become a squad leader. And I want to wear gold insignia and march next to my squad, marking time!'

But my Uncle had said that I was both *piccola* and *italiana* and that should be more than enough, and that he wasn't particularly keen on me wearing gold insignia anyway. He would much rather I just stop telling lies. Then he'd told Cosimo to take us to school.

The party officer asked, 'Who are you?'

The teacher explained I was the Master's niece and the officer's expression suddenly changed. He said, 'Send my regards to your uncle.'

The chauffeur came to pick us up and our car drew away from the crowd of waving children, leaving a trail of dust in its wake.

I brought the fascist officer's regards to my uncle.

(13)

Yesterday I didn't do anything wrong, but today I tore my dress. So I ran to find Elsa in the kitchen and told her to sew it back up on the spot. Elsa sewed it up for me but just as she was finishing, Uncle came in and asked me what I was doing in the kitchen.

I said I was thirsty, which was a lie, but then he asked if I had broken a pane in the dining room window. I said that it hadn't been me.

At the table later, Marie wanted to know if anyone had seen her ball of red wool and before I had time to kick her in the shins, Baby blurted out that we'd borrowed it to play catch.

Uncle's face became serious.

'And where did you play catch?'

'Outside,' I said.

'But I found the wool in the dining room,' said Marie, looking very angry. 'I've told you countless times not to touch other people's things. So why did you say you were playing outside?'

Annie started to laugh.

'I meant to say inside,' I insisted.

'So why did you say outside?'

'Because we were pretending to be outside when we were in the dining room.'

'Alright, but since the glass fish is also broken that means you were in the drawing room as well as the dining room.'

'Yes, but we thought we were in the garden.'

After Uncle had scolded me and sent me to bed without my dinner, I wondered what I had done to deserve such harsh words.

Yes, the window was broken and the glass fish was too. But was there glass in the woods? Or glass fish in the air? How was it my fault they'd been broken? We hadn't done it on purpose, Baby and I. Baby had decided that the drawing room was the garden, and the dining room the courtyard. How was it my fault if for Uncle a drawing room was just a drawing room and a fish just a fish?

We hadn't been thinking of the fish as a fish but as an Englishman who was standing on the hillside and whom we had to shoot. He had died when the Piccole Italiane and the Balilla had conquered the hill.

It wasn't true that I had no brain and no heart. Besides, it was the Duce's fault: he'd broken the fish because the Duce was also in the drawing room, fighting by our side.

What did Annie have to laugh about, anyway? I was just glad she got a telling off from Uncle too, because none of us were allowed to laugh at the table when Uncle was angry.

Meanwhile, I was waiting for the day Uncle would understand that I was good and that my truth was true. I could already picture him coming to me with open arms, wanting to make peace and to give me all the kisses and cuddles he'd been holding back for so long.

(14)

Today we went into the kitchen where Marie was making whipped cream cornets for Annie's birthday but she shooed us away and so we went outside to play *corsaro nero*.

Lorenza Mazzetti

I always played the black corsair. Annie always wanted to play the corsair's wife so that she could put on lipstick, while Baby liked to play the corsair's friend.

Whenever Annie wasn't up for playing, Baby and I would play Don Quixote and Sancho Panza, as there were just two of us. The game consisted of us battling against the windmills on our horses. I led the way and Baby followed. I would wear a dish on my head for a helmet and we would ride on the back of our Saint Bernard dog, Alì, with brooms in our hands.

Uncle had given us *Don Quixote* for Christmas.

Later that day, Uncle gave us a book called *The Head Hunters*, so we all decided to attack Mister Pit. At first Mister Pit defended himself but after a while he just let us get on with it, assuming his habitual air of superiority and acting as if he thought we were just fooling around. But I for sure wasn't fooling around, and we tied him tight to the trunk of a tree, winding a rope all the way around his body. And because he'd also lost his glasses he couldn't see properly, so he couldn't escape.

I came up with the idea that we should ask him for a ransom and demanded he give us all the sweets he had in his pockets and hidden in his bedroom.

Uncle hadn't spoken to me in three days. How could I get him to speak to me again?

I told myself that one day I would run far away from this house where no one hugged or kissed me. Everyone would be happier without me and Elsa would no longer scream that I was bothering her in the kitchen or that her chicken was missing (I only took it to feed the poor stray dog that Baby and I had found) and Marie would no longer scream because

I told Leonardo she was in love with him (I read it in her diary so how was it a lie? No, I told the truth, and I was punished for it.)

And Annie would no longer be angry at me, because I would no longer be around to steal her yellow teddy bear that I liked so much, even though one of its eyes was missing. I'd taken its eye out and given it to Ginetta to help ward off the evil eye (someone had put a curse on Tosca, Ginetta's sister, and she had stopped eating.)

Even Baby would be better off without me. But how would I get by without Baby? True, I was stronger than her and I could survive on figs and grapes and work to earn a living. Then no one would be able to call me 'ungrateful' ever again.

Grown-ups believed that children didn't suffer. They thought that I had no heart because the day before, when Uncle had told me to fetch him his glasses to read the mail, I had dropped them as I was running and they'd broken. But wasn't it always the case that I ran as fast as lighting as soon as a grown up needed something?

Penny, go and fetch Uncle's cane; Penny, go upstairs and get the chess set; Penny, go and fetch my glasses; Penny, go up and get my sun hat. Even Annie took me for her personal servant: Penny, go and fetch the bowling set for the lawn. They screamed at me all the time. If only they knew what dark thoughts came into my mind when they spoke to me like that! They didn't even know that I had often considered suicide.

If I had died then everybody would have loved me and Aunt Katchen would've brought me cookies and Elsa a warm mug of broth and Uncle would've let me stay in his bed between him and Aunt Katchen. They would have held me tight, and I would have been so happy. I would have cried from too much happiness.

So I'd written on a piece of paper *I'm going to hang myself*, and then I'd hanged myself but since I never died I hid in the Villa's attic with the rope still around my neck. From up there, I could see Uncle, Elsa, Baby, and Annie running from left to right and up and down the big staircase, hurrying from room to room, along with Marie, who was crying, and Mister Pit.

I'd always believed that Marie was like the Madonnina, that she was good and truly loved me. Elsa, on the other hand, was evil. 'That stupid girl,' I could hear her say, 'This is just another of her stupid games!' Baby wasn't crying because she knew I was up in the attic. I felt sorry for Uncle and when he called my name I suddenly felt like weeping. Could it be true that he wanted me back?

I began to feel nervous about going back downstairs without having successfully hanged myself. The rope was still around my neck, but I wasn't quite sure where to hang myself from.

Aunt Katchen, in tears, shouted, 'Penny! Come back!' And because she was crying and so was Marie, and because Uncle and all the others, even Mister Pit, were outside calling my name, I decided to come downstairs.

Uncle looked me straight in the eye without saying a word. Aunt Katchen was crying.

'Why did you do that?' she asked, hugging me. 'Aren't you happy living here with us?'

Then I burst into tears, too, and told her how much I loved her and Uncle and that I thought they didn't love me anymore because I was bad. And I said that Uncle never hugged me, and I climbed onto his lap and my tears fell down his neck. He hugged me tight. Then he punished me by sending me to bed without any dinner.

I love Uncle Wilhelm more than the Duce, more than Jesus and more than our country, Italy.

(15)

There was going to be a play at our school. We were all going to perform in it. Elsa was making our costumes with Rosa's help. Baby was going to be dressed as an angel and so was I. Marie and Katchen were making her wings. They were making a pair for me, too, even though Marie said my eyes were too wicked for an angel. The teacher had asked Annie and Marie to play the violin and Baby and I to sing a new fascist hymn. Uncle hated it when we sang this song and always hurried out of the drawing room whenever we practised it with Marie and Annie accompanying us on piano and violin. Annie put on a lot of airs because she knew how to play the violin. Whenever she was asked to go upstairs to fetch Aunty's spectacles (she was always forgetting them) or to do any other equally boring job, she'd say, 'You two go, I have to practise the violin'. But she never really did. It was all just a ploy to ride her bicycle.

Baby and I decided we were going to beat her up with all our might.

Admittedly, it was hard for us to play angels with these thoughts in our heads. Serenella and Piera

Cuccurullo – *they* would be good at playing angels, with all that hair flowing down their shoulders. They were in the third year. My hair was short and dark. How I would have liked to have long straight hair, too!

Fabrizia, who was in the fourth year, was going to play the part of the Madonna, and behind her all the angels would sing in chorus. Some of the girls would be sitting on benches. Others would wear garlands on their heads. I was going to be in the second row, on the right. I too would wear a garland on my head, but Baby was going to stand in the front row with a lily in her hand. When the teacher gave us a sign, we would begin to sing. The party officer was going to be in the audience. Annie, who was taller than me, would be dressed as a Piccola Italiana.

The chorus was quite complicated because it was the part that all the angels sang, and it went higher and higher until I couldn't hit the right notes. We'd sing *Ave Maria* when the officer gave us his sign, then the fascist hymn, and afterwards all the angels would stand up, pass the lily from their right to left hands, and raise their arms in the Roman salute. Even Marie was going to dress up as a woman from Ancient Rome, holding a sheaf of wheat in her arms to represent the goddess Ceres and the abundance of Italy.

(16)

Our maid Rosa made love to Nello in the woods, and Pippone made love to Beppa.

'What do they do when they make love?'

Zeffirino said Pippone made love every night behind the bushes and that if I wanted to see, he would take me there. Beppa was Cencetti's wife and they had five children, one of whom was nicknamed Corpoliscio because he had a very smooth body.

'How do you make love?'

Zeffirino said it didn't take much, that it really was a very simple thing.

When we reached the top of the hill to look for Pippone, the sun was already setting. The tree trunks were red on the side of the sunset and black on the other. I'd taken my shoes off like Zefferino and when I put my ear to the ground as he did, I could hear distant noises coming from beyond the gorse bushes.

'Let's go and take a look.'

We went up to the bush where they were making love. I saw that a man was lying on top of a woman. I understood this because he had four feet, though their heads were hidden by the bushes.

'They're so still they must be dead!'

'Pippone has four legs!' Zeffirino said and burst out laughing until a stone hit him in the head and shut him up at once. We started to race down the hill. I'd seen Pippone rise from the bushes, screaming and tossing stones at us. He was still standing at the top of the hill like a giant, throwing little rocks into the distance.

'Did you see?' said Zeffirino, red in the face, once we had reached the bottom, 'They were kissing!'

Baby and Pasquetta and Lea and Pierino were out in the courtyard.

'We saw Pippone and Beppa making love!'

'Reeeally?' they all asked in unison.

'They were kissing!'

'What do they do when they kiss?' asked Baby.

'They touch their tongues together.'

'Pippone and Beppa touch tongues?'

'Yes, yes, they touch tongues,' said Zeffirino, 'I've seen them with my own eyes.'

'Do they also touch tongues when they make love?'

Pierino said that the spots you could see on the moon were two lovers kissing. 'Haven't you seen what the lovers on the moon are doing?'

'No,' said Baby.

'Let me show you.' Pierino stuck out his tongue and told Lea to stick out hers and they stood facing each other and touched tongues. Lea jumped backwards in a fit of laughter, saying Pierino had tickled her nose.

'Me too! Me too!' said Baby.

'Here I come...' said Pierino, crouching down to Baby's height. Pierino and Baby touched tongues, then Pasquetta and Lea touched tongues, then Zeffirino and I stood in front of each other to kiss. But then we started making faces and taking swipes at each other, and Pierino kissed me by licking my whole face and neck. Zeffirino also began to lick my ears and we all slipped and sank in the wheat.

'I'm full of lice!' yelled Zeffirino.

'One more kiss!'

'I'm going to catch you!'

Laughing, we began to make our way across the field of wheat, which was almost as tall as Baby. All of a sudden I spotted Pierino's father on the other side of the field, screaming at us to stop crushing his harvest.

(17)

The local party officer came to see our play. Then Baby and I, dressed as angels, stepped forward to sing the song dedicated to the Duce. It went like this:

Mussolini, Mussolini, with his cane and his cannon, with his bold and proudest semblance, Fascism and Nation shall triumph all!

Then Annie came forward dressed as a Piccola Italiana, holding her violin in her hand. Our teacher was on the brink of tears and had gone completely red. Annie was red too and her hand was shaking. She began to play but she was so nervous she couldn't read the score. So Baby and I started singing at the top of our lungs, so loudly that the party officer couldn't hear that Annie was playing out of key. But since Annie was playing off-key, we started singing out of key too.

'Viva il Duce!' our teacher shouted, as the party officer was getting ready to leave.

'Long may he live!' we all shouted at the top of our lungs. But the party officer came back to question us. He made Zeffirino step forward and asked him, 'What is the longest river in Italy?'

Zeffirino thought about this for a while, then Cesira whispered, 'Ppp...ppp...'

'The car!' said Zeffirino.

'The Po!' said the party officer, angrily. He turned to interrogate Cesira.

'What kind of animal is a camel?' the party officer asked.

The teacher smiled at Cesira to encourage her. She had actually taught us about camels recently and we'd even had to write a short essay about them. But Cesira replied that camels live in the desert and said that when they got hungry they ate their own lumps, instead of saying that they ate their own humps.

When we returned to the Villa, Uncle let us keep our angel costumes on for the day.

*

The procession of the Madonna was planned for Sunday. The peasants would carry her on their shoulders from the village church to the Villa, then back again. They would walk with the Madonna on their shoulders and tip her forwards every five steps to greet the crowd. The women would sing *Ave, ave Maria*. The trouble was that Pasquetta and Lea sang so loudly that the priest said they sounded like barking dogs.

On Sunday, the priest announced that the Bishop was coming to the village. Lea was the one to tell me about the visit because we weren't allowed to go to Mass. She said that the Bishop would come and see Uncle at the Villa.

'The Bishop wears a ring that works miracles and you have to kiss his hand.'

'So the Bishop will come to the Villa just to see Uncle?' Baby asked.

Lea said it would be as if the Holy Spirit were entering our house and repeated that the Bishop wore a gigantic ring that could work miracles. Baby said she didn't ever want the Bishop to leave the villa if that meant him taking his blessing away with him.

She worried about whether she'd have enough time to line up all her toys in order to receive the Bishop's blessing.

'How come the Bishop is visiting Uncle if he's not even baptised?'

'Maybe the Bishop doesn't know that.'

The Villa had been decked out for the occasion and colourful rugs had been hung from the windows. Katchen and Marie busied themselves arranging them in each room. As usual, Uncle had shut himself in his study with his books. He was more irritable than usual and I had already been told off a few times. Everyone was running around and chattering.

We little ones were sent into the fields to pick flowers to arrange into a bright carpet at the bottom of the stone steps that led up to the Villa, where the procession would set the Madonna down for a moment before carrying her off again.

A light breeze lifted Baby's dress up as she bent down to pick flowers for the Madonna. Soon she disappeared among the gorse and the poppies. Every so often her blonde curls reappeared and she came skipping back to me with little handfuls of violets and cyclamens.

The peasants had spelled out 'Ave Maria' on the avenue with laurel leaves. We were given the task of filling in the empty sections with flowers. The letter 'A' was all yellow with gorse and the letter 'M' was purple and red with violets and poppies. Elsa was calling us. 'Come up and get dressed!'

She sent us back downstairs, all cleaned up with ribbons in our hair. You could see the procession coming up the hill. The Carabinieri were at its head, followed by the priest who gave out his blessings, and then by his altar boys, the party officer, singing women and children dressed all in white, including Pasquetta. She looked like a different girl dressed like that. She sang and didn't even look at us. And then, there he was, the Bishop... And then, and then... the Madonna!

Beneath her golden canopy, the Madonna slowly approached the Villa on the shoulders of men, bowing every few steps to greet the crowd.

'Look at the Madonna, she's crying!' said Zeffirino.

'She smiled at us!' Lea shouted.

She approached us very slowly. At the bottom of the grand staircase stood Uncle, dressed in white and wearing his white wide-brimmed hat.

'He could be a saint,' said Pasquetta, looking at him.

'If the Madonna grants him grace, he will be.'

The trumpets sounded and everyone sang even more loudly.

The Madonna bowed one final time, then turned and began heading back, until she disappeared at the end of the avenue, followed by the procession.

'She waved at me! Did she wave at you?'

'She didn't.' I said, sadly.

(18)

Marie was very anxious. She was preparing strawberries to serve to the Bishop. Marie was good at preparing the strangest dishes. Today she had decided to whip up a strawberry mousse.

'Katchen, are you ready?'

Uncle always spoke in English, unless he was angry, in which case he spoke in German.

He told me to call Aunt Katchen because it was getting late. Aunt Katchen sent me to the kitchen to see if Marie was ready, taking the opportunity to pinch my nose as a thank you and to ask me a few questions in English. The butler was pacing up and down and it was getting on my nerves. He looked down on us as if he were the master of the house.

All the servants and the peasants were crammed into the hallway, waiting for the chance to kiss the Bishop's hand. Finally, the Bishop's car pulled up.

Out came the village priest, a friar, another priest, and then the Bishop, dressed head to toe in purple. The parish priest led the way. Uncle walked up to them and held out his hand.

Baby and Annie and I waited in the hallway with all the servants and the peasants who wanted to kiss the Bishop's hand. The Bishop looked very grand and I thought I could see a special light in his eyes. Everyone threw themselves at his feet, kissing his hand. He smiled sweetly, with a look of great kindness, as he held out his bejewelled hand. He offered his hand to Baby. Baby clung to it and wouldn't let go. The Bishop shook his hand and then his arm, his face, and began to frown. Baby clung to his hand and sobbed, 'Save him! Save him!' We couldn't understand much more than that. Once more, the Bishop violently shook his hand, without managing to get rid of Baby. I saw Uncle come forward, looking angry. He said, 'Baby! What are you doing?'

We all yanked Baby off the Bishop's hand and he began to smile again, following the others into the drawing room.

The Bishop's mantle had been left in the hallway and the peasants began to kiss it.

'Birdbrain!' said Lea to Baby.

Between sobs, Baby said that because Uncle hadn't kissed the Bishop's ring he wouldn't be saved. She didn't want the Bishop to leave the Villa without working a miracle.

'So long as the Bishop is in the Villa,' said Pasquetta, all dressed in white with a strip of silk wrapped around her head, 'the Holy Spirit resides here,' and she nodded towards the Bishop's mantle hanging in the hallway.

I snuck out into the garden and peeked through the slats of the drawing room shutters, which were ajar. I heard the priest ask Uncle why he wouldn't send us to Mass, since we had been baptised and it was surely what our parents would have wanted.

Uncle replied, in a rather cold voice, that he wanted to let us decide for ourselves once we were old enough to understand.

And though the parish priest said that it just wasn't right that we didn't go to Mass, the Bishop interjected, talking about the infinite goodness of God and how sooner or later it would illuminate everything. The Bishop spoke sweetly, like a saint.

Cosimo came in with the strawberries.

I saw Baby come running into the garden from the hallway. I could see a piece of cloth in her hands – purple, just like the Bishop's mantle.

'I cut off a piece of his mantle!' Baby said. 'Now the Holy Spirit can't ever leave our home.' And using the scissors she held in her other hand, she began digging into the earth below the medlar tree.

'I'll bury it here,' she said.

THE SKY IS FALLING   101

That evening, Uncle sent us to bed with no dinner and I had to fill twenty pages with the line: *I will never cut off a piece of a Bishop's cloak again.*

(19)

The bell rang and I ran downstairs to find Baby, who was making Zeffirino carry her school bag.

'Look!' said Baby, sticking out her tongue.

'Baby, look at me!' said Pierino, sticking out his own. 'Which one is longer?'

'Penny, show me yours.'

I stuck out my tongue but Zeffirino won because he was able to touch the tip of his nose.

'Come, young ladies, the car is here!'

As we drove home, we heard a sound like distant thunder.

'Is it raining?' Baby asked the chauffeur.

'No. That's the sound of cannons.'

I had been very sad because the King had put the Duce in jail. But then his friend Hitler came and saved him, and now the Duce was speaking out against traitors on the radio.

I no longer recognised his voice because he was no longer speaking about victory but resistance. I remembered the speech he'd once given from Palazzo Venezia. The voice on the radio had said:

Behold the Duce, surveying his troops. Behold the Duce: he doesn't walk, he soars. Behold the Duce: he has finished surveying his soldiers and is walking with a proud step towards his officials, who can barely keep up with him. The Duce's feet scarcely touch the ground and his gaze is bold. He smiles as he begins to ascend the stairs, and the officials can hardly follow him, his step is so agile! Behold, now the Duce has reached the balcony. He steps out to greet the jubilant crowd!

But today Uncle sat listening in his chair with a frown on his face.

How well the Duce spoke. His voice had such a rich sound. He spoke at regular intervals, which were interrupted by the cries of the crowd:

Because Fascist Italy...

He shouted.

I say, Fascist Italy...

He shouted.

Will not be defeated. We shall triumph!

He shouted.

We started shouting too.

'Long live Italy!' Annie screamed, flustered.

'Long live the Duce! Long live Italy!' Baby and I shouted.

'Shall we hang the Italian flag from the window, Papà?' Annie said.

Uncle didn't answer.

Annie frowned, turning towards Marie and Katchen, 'The flag, Mamma!'

'Get out of here!' Uncle yelled, suddenly serious, 'You're being too loud!'

The three of us ran into the courtyard singing fascist hymns at the top of our lungs. How I wished the Duce could hear us and know that we were on his side, that he could count on us, that we were proud to be Piccole Italiane and willing if necessary to give our blood for the cause of the fascist revolution.

Once at school the party officer had told us that the Duce had liberated Italy from the Bolsheviks who wore red shirts, took God's name in vain, and always spat on the ground.

'Wanna play war?' Pierino said later that afternoon.

'I'll be the General. Who are you?' I asked.

'I'm Fabio Fabrucci from the Third Infantry Regiment,' said Pierino.

'Captain, I thank you for your heroic deeds. Did you find the enemy?'

'Yessir, I saw him and surrounded him from behind.'

'You did? Without being seen?'

'Yessir.'

'Where are the prisoners?'

'Here they are, Mister General.'

They came with their hands up, one after the other: first Baby, then Zeffirino, Lea, Pasquetta, and Angelo.

'Put your hands down,' I said in the voice of the General.

'Goddamn the goddamn English!' Pierino shouted.

'And now, Captain, tell us about your heroic deeds.'

'It went like this, Mister General. I was standing guard when I spotted the enemy. I said to myself, Uh oh, there's the enemy!'

'How did you know it was the enemy?'

'Mister General, you told me.'

'Don't you know all enemies wear red shirts and are Bolsheviks?'

'Yessir, and they all curse God.'

'Did you tell them not to blaspheme and spit on the ground?'

'Yessir, I told them not to blaspheme.'

'Alright. And then what did you do?'

'After I took the enemy captive, I took the Italian flag and planted it on top of the mountain, shouting *Viva il Duce*, sir.'

'Bravo.'

'Let's give him a medal.'

'Alright, here's a medal.'

'Good morning, Mister General,' said Zeffirino, stepping forward.

'Who are you?'

'Private Alfiero Brissoni of the Sixth Infantry.'

'What do you want?'

'I snuck into the enemy camp, sir, and without being seen I stole their chickens and planted the tricolore in place of the enemy flag. As I was escaping, I killed the enemy commander with my bayonet and his aide with a blow to the back of the head, and the rest of the soldiers with this little bag of poison I'd been keeping right here in my shirt pocket. Then I had to wrestle down the guard who was about to raise the alarm. So I stuck my bayonet right through his heart and he went down going *urghhhh!* Next, I turned around and saw that ten more enemies were about to attack me from behind and *whack! whack!* I killed them all. He fell to the ground but then he tried to get back at me – he took out my eye, Mister General. I gave it up gladly for the Fatherland.'

'Alright, here's your medal.'

Then came Pierino. He staggered forward on crutches.

'What are those?'

'They're crutches, Mister General.'

'What happened?'

'War, Mister General.'

Pierino was trembling as he spoke, rhythmically shaking his head.

'Are you hurt?'

'It doesn't matter, Mister General.'

'You are a brave man. Tell us all about it.'

'I was hitting... Left, right... A head here, a head there...'

'How many are dead?'

'Not a soul, Mister General.'

'You're a brave man.'

'Me too! Me too!'

Baby, Annie, Zeffirino, and the rest were shouting, some limping, others pretending to carry broken arms in slings hanging down from their necks.

'Quiet, you!'

'Baccucci Fiorenzo, soldier, Fifth Cavalry Regiment.'

'How did you lose your legs?'

'It went like this, Mister General. It was dark and I couldn't see, but I heard the voice of the enemy saying, "All Italians are pigs!" So I said, "You're the pigs!" And I threw myself at them and killed them all. Then one of them said, "You're a brave Italian pig." And even though I had already lost my legs by this point, I dragged myself over to the window, and hung the tricolore. Then, still with no legs, I came back here, Mister General. At your command!'

'Alright. Here's your medal.'

'Long live the Duce! Down with the English! Forwards, attack!'

We sprung forward, running and screaming *ra-ta-ta-tat*.

The following day our chauffeur suddenly pulled on the brakes in the middle of the road. We climbed out of the car to see what was happening. A bunch of singing fascists were passing by. They were dressed all in black, with black boots and golden insignia. Their lips were covered by their bushy moustaches.

'Come along, young ladies,' said the chauffeur. He bundled us back into the car and drove us up to the Villa.

In the courtyard, Pippone grabbed Baby by her feet and threw her up into the air before catching her again. He went for a little stroll, carrying Baby and me under his arms like two burlap sacks.

Pippone said, 'My pockets are so big they could fit two ships inside: one in the left, one in the right.'

'Really?'

'Of course. Two ships,' he repeated.

'Annie, did you know that Pippone has two ships in his pockets?'

'Stupid girl.'

'Annie, can I ride your bicycle for a bit?'

'You'll break it!'

'No, I won't break it. Annie, let me ride your bicycle, just for a little bit!'

'You and Baby break everything.'

'I'll do anything you want,' I pleaded, 'if you let me have a go on your bicycle.'

Annie paused for a moment, thinking. Then she said, 'If you make me Queen, I'll give it to you.'

Pasquetta, Lea, Zeffirino and Pierino all wanted to try Annie's bicycle too, and so we made her Queen.

We all attended Annie's coronation ceremony. How I hated her then, sitting up on her throne and ordering Lea to comb her hair while the rest of us bowed and got on our hands and knees in front of her. We'd become her slaves. Only Lea had earned the Queen's confidence and become her advisor.

'Stinkyfeet!' Pasquetta shouted to her.

'You're the one who stinks!' said Lea to Pasquetta and whacked her on the head.

'Stop it!' said the Queen, descending from her throne. 'I want you to shout a hundred times: *Long live Annie*!'

We shouted *long live Annie* a hundred times but it still wasn't enough. We had to cover ourselves in mud, crawl on our knees, and do her every kind of service imaginable. First of all, we had to brush her hair. Then I had to give over all my pinecones to the Queen. Until one day I snapped: 'You know what? Keep your bicycle!'

We'd invented a new game anyway: riding wild pigs. Pierino's mother let the pigs free in the morning and they came back of their own accord in the evening. During the day they went off into the woods to eat chestnuts. Wild pigs, said Lea, were able to crack open chestnuts with their noses and eat the insides without hurting themselves on the sharp shells. She said that they were wild animals and that when they were eaten they were called *magroni*. We also ate the raw chestnuts we found in the woods, even though they gave us tummy aches.

'Aaaaaagh!' Pierino screamed, leaping on a passing pig. Most of the time we were thrown off with a grunt. It was best to hold onto their tails or ears. Oh, how wonderful it was to gallop through the woods brushing against the grass, holding onto a pig's ears! The only problem was that afterwards Baby and I would stink.

One day Zeffirino turned up completely bald.

'Had nits,' he said and threw himself on the nearest pig. We all followed suit, screaming. Each of us on our own pig, squeezing their bodies with our knees and whipping them to make them run even faster.

(21)

We were reciting the Ten Commandments and I wondered what it meant to fornicate. Pasquetta said it meant you shouldn't speak ill of God. But I was also confused by the part that said, 'Thou shalt not covet thy neighbour's wife.' It had never crossed my mind to go after someone else's wife, whereas I'd often wanted to go after someone else's bicycle. But then I thought that if my wish for a bicycle were to be granted, it would have felt like a waste, because I could have asked for my neighbour's wife after all.

Pasquetta had just been confirmed. The Bishop had stuck a nail into her forehead and wrapped a strip of silk around it. This was why she'd been acting cocky, as if she were somewhat above us because we'd not been confirmed yet.

'Everything is ready for Mass.'

We were holding a service for Uncle.

We had built a church in the woods so that Baby and I could attend Mass on Sundays. We all knelt before the altar. We took the chocolate squares we'd stopped ourselves from eating in order to save Uncle out of their tin box, and then we placed them on the altar. Zeffirino had brought some chicken.

To make our suffering worse, we'd gathered some sharp stones to kneel on for the time it took us to say the rosary. Pasquetta pulled out a figurine of the Madonna in a light blue dress and pink mantle. She said she'd tried to lick the statuette and that it tasted like sugar. We all licked the statuette that tasted like sugar. Beneath her, we put one photograph of Uncle and one of the Duce.

Lea said that Saint Theresa used to whip herself every day before the Cross and that Saint Francis had slept on the ground, even when he was sick and all the other friars were saying, "Come on then, Francis, we want you to get better, you must get into bed!" But Saint Francis said no, he wouldn't sleep in his bed, he wanted to sleep on the hard ground, and he died peacefully there. We decided that we, too, should scourge ourselves and sleep on the ground. Pierino went off looking for a suitable stick and came back with a whip made of reeds.

'Whip me!' I said.

Baby said, 'Whip me too!' and she got into position, sticking her bum out. She covered her ears with her hands so she wouldn't be able to hear how much it hurt. Pierino whipped us all as we lay on our fronts with our dresses pulled up over our heads. He whipped us very earnestly. I received five lashes.

'Five! As many as our Lord Jesus Christ's holy wounds!'

'Do you repent?'

'Yes,' Pasquetta said.

Pierino began to whip Pasquetta so hard that she lunged back at him and bit him.

Then Pierino gave the whip to Zeffirino.

'Do you repent?' Zeffirino shouted, raising the whip.

'Yes,' said Baby.

'And one!' said Zeffirino, bringing the whip down on her.

'Do you repent?'

'Yes.'

'And two!'

When the whip hit her, Baby screamed, 'Holy Madonna!'

'Do you repent?' Zeffirino asked her again.

'Yes!'

'And three! And four!'

'Ouch! Ouch' said Baby, looking down at her red-dened thighs.

'Do you repent?' asked Zeffirino, raising the whip again.

'Yes!' said Baby, getting back into position. 'Ouch, ouch, Holy Madonna!'

Then Pierino grabbed the whip and began to brandish it right and left as if he wanted to kill us all.

(22)

Nello had asked Rosa to wait by the crossroads, but he hadn't come. That evening, Rosa was crying because it was a Sunday and she'd dressed up for the occasion in her tightest dress, and I'd curled her hair and pinned a rose to her chest. All of this for Nello. But Nello had spent that evening at the village osteria playing cards with Pippone and the others, and he'd called Mussolini a pig. I really didn't understand why Nello had it in for our Duce.

Ferruccio reported the fact that Nello had called Mussolini a pig to the Party. Rosa insisted he'd actually been saying *Viva il Duce* but I didn't believe her because I'd heard Nello say bad things about Mussolini with my very own ears and it had upset me. If Mussolini had heard them, it would have made him very sad.

Ferruccio arrived at the Villa the following day in a black car full of men in black fascist uniforms. They led Nello out of the courtyard and into the woods.

I thought maybe I didn't love Mussolini so much anymore because you were meant to forgive your neighbour and instead he'd sent his men to get Nello, and they'd come and taken him to the woods. Lea said they'd formed a circle around him and beat him with their sticks. Lea said that his screams could be heard all the way from her house but that her father had been too scared to go out.

Rosa, on the other hand, had run into the woods shouting, 'Stop, stop!' but they caught her and, with great relish, held her back by her arms, covering her mouth and making her watch as they beat up Nello. Maybe the Duce didn't know about Ferruccio beating up Nello. I decided to write him a letter:

Dear Duce,

I've decided to write to let you know what happened to my friend Nello, who was beaten black and blue by Ferruccio because he says that Nello said porco Duce, *which isn't true anyway because Nello always says* Viva

Mussolini. *I have heard him say it with my very own ears, it's just that Ferruccio is jealous of Nello because of Rosa, and so I beg you to do something because I love you very much and I'm a Piccola Italiana and a squad leader at the Rosa Maltoni school.*

PENNY AND BABY

Uncle told me to give him the letter and he would have it posted. But the Duce must have been so busy with the war that he never had a chance to reply. The enemy was getting closer.

(23)

One morning I decided to go and watch the sun rise. Baby was sleeping so I left the room on tiptoe, went out and climbed a tree. In the silence of dawn, I could distinctly hear the roar of the cannons, which sounded closer than usual. The sun was rising slowly to my right. I listened to the sounds of different insects as I watched a line of caterpillars climb the trunk of the tree in which I was perched.

My knees had acquired a red colour in the light cast by the rising sun. I'd never seen a dawn before because they didn't wake us children up until eight at the Villa. I wondered if the sun really was yellow or if it was yellow only for me. Perhaps Uncle, who was a Jew, saw it as blue or green...

I pursed my lips like Pierino and began to imitate the birds. Shifting my weight from the right branch to the left, I managed to keep my balance, and I thought about how without balance birds would not be able to fly and fish would not be able to swim. By holding onto a branch with my right hand and the trunk with my left while gripping the branch beneath me with my feet, I could stay in my tree for a very long time.

I started to count the leaves on the tree and by the time I had counted nearly all of them, it was almost midday. From where I was, I could see the Villa and hear Baby calling my name. I heard the sound of car brakes. A strange, blotchily-painted vehicle had pulled up in front of the stone steps. A German soldier got out and opened the door for an officer. Then he stood to attention, snapping his boots together.

The officer climbed up the stone steps and rang the bell. Alì barked. Elsa came to open the door. I watched her disappear, leaving the officer there on the doorstep with the door ajar. She came back with Marie, and I saw that they were talking. Marie could speak German. The officer stepped into the hallway and Marie closed the door behind him.

I was so curious that I climbed down from my tree and made my way back to the Villa.

'Penny! What are you doing?'

'I want to have a look in the salon.'

We clung to the big wrought iron bars that protected the windows on the ground floor of the Villa. Hoisting myself up, I saw the German officer completely alone in the salon with the mirrors hanging behind him. I felt tired so I hopped off to tell Baby. Suddenly notes were coming from the piano. They grew louder and began to echo throughout the Villa.

'It's Beethoven's sonata! The one Uncle always plays!'

I pulled myself up onto the railings again and saw that the German officer was sitting at the grand piano and playing it. He played for a long time, almost an hour and a half. He must've given orders to be picked up later because the same car came back, stopping once more at the foot of the steps.

Marie said that the officer had come to the Villa with the specific purpose of asking permission to play the piano after he'd heard its notes from afar. Uncle had sent the butler to say yes, but he forbade Marie and us to speak to the guest.

The officer came back the next day at the same time. He was let into the salon and left alone. The notes did not begin immediately. The officer was waiting for something before he began his concert. Perhaps it was Marie? After nearly half an hour of silence, he began to play. After an hour and a half, the car came to pick him up. Before he left the officer lifted his head and saw us and Marie spying on him through the half-closed shutters.

The following day the officer was five minutes late. Those five minutes felt like an eternity to me, as if the Villa had been plunged back into silence. All the guests had left a long time ago because of the war. Edith and her husband had returned to Zurich, and Uncle's cousin 'Maya' had gone to America to stay with her brother, who was a famous scientist at Princeton. No longer able to have fun at Mister Pit's expense or watch Edith paint, Baby and I took refuge in a new love.

No longer able to love Leonardo, we set out to love Lieutenant Friedrich.

I realised that I was waiting for Lieutenant Friedrich to arrive just as I'd waited for Leonardo.

What a strange thing love is. I'd never have imagined that I could be in love with Lieutenant Friedrich in the same way I'd been in love with Leonardo. What amazed me even more was the fact that Marie and Annie and Baby were all in love with him too.

There was nothing that could be done about it: all women were frivolous and shallow, just like the priest had said, and guilty of the sin of adultery.

The next time the officer came, he brought a bunch of roses with him. He asked the butler if it was possible to see the *schöne Fraulein* who had opened the door to him the first time he visited.

Marie appeared at the threshold of the salon looking very shy. She curtsied and thanked him for the flowers before quickly disappearing again. Uncle wouldn't allow her to stay in the room with the officer. He had begun spending even more time in his study among his books and his face was increasingly drawn.

The officer came back several times. We spied on him through the bushes, but we didn't dare speak to him because Uncle had forbidden it.

(24)

I was walking to the creek when I spotted lots of soldiers bathing. They had blue eyes and blonde hair. How different they were from us Italians, who were so much darker! And how entertaining it was to have all these new neighbours at the Villa! There were a lot of comings and goings. Cars and soldiers.

To my and Baby's great delight, sometimes the soldiers even came up to the Villa. Even the General came along, sending a note to Uncle through his aide, Hainz, in which he offered his heartfelt apologies for the inconvenience and begged Uncle to forgive his intrusion, but unfortunately *la guerre c'est la guerre* and he, the General, was in need of some rooms.

Uncle locked himself away in his study, his face darker than ever, after giving the General permission to occupy the guest rooms while his soldiers invaded the granary and the mill.

Soldiers went up and down the stairs, their boots making a real racket. The corridors rang with shouts. It was the soldiers, snapping to attention.

At five o'clock on the dot, as usual, Lieutenant Friedrich began playing the piano. Then somebody else appeared on the threshold of the salon and I couldn't believe my eyes... It was the General himself!

'The General is sitting in the armchair and listening,' I said, sliding down from the railings. Pierino climbed up and took my place.

'The General is listening to the music... Now he's smoking a cigarette...'

'But what's he doing now?'

'Now he's standing up and walking around... Now he's leaving.'

Unlike the ones we'd had before, so far our new guests had been completely ignored by Uncle. The butler never came into the salon to serve coffee to the General or to Lieutenant Friederich, and Uncle never invited them to lunch. Instead it was the soldiers who sent messages to Uncle, mostly thank you notes for letting them use the piano.

'If Uncle won't be kind to the General then we will be kind for him,' I said.

'How?'

'Let me think.'

'You know that Uncle doesn't want us to talk to them. We're not meant to go into their rooms or touch any of the cannons or machine guns without his permission,' said Baby.

'You know what I'm thinking? If Uncle's going to be mean to the guests, we'll need to do the honours of the house ourselves.'

'Penny's talking rubbish again.'

'Actually, this time she's right.'

'Let's invite the General to lunch.'

There were soldiers all around the Villa getting their mess tins ready as it approached one in the afternoon. We, on the other hand, were standing at the top of the avenue among the laurels, putting the final touches to the magnificent lunch we had prepared for the General. Pierino had made soup and there was even dessert. More and more soldiers were arriving, carrying cannons and machine guns. We stood at the top of the avenue, cooking lunch with our dolls. Pasquetta had made a fire and was preparing a broth made with a little water, a little earth, a pinch of pine needles and a garnish of chopped leaves.

Finally, the General's car arrived, leaving a cloud of dust in its wake.

'*Il generale!*' said Pierino.

The General got out of the car. He was tall and wide with silver insignia and badges on his hat. It was hot. He must have been tired. He walked down the avenue and handed some papers over to his aide, Hainz, who snapped to attention. It was hot. The General took off his hat and wiped his forehead.

'We have to do something!'

The General was giving orders to his soldiers. He looked worried and irritated. Even Generals sometimes lose their temper.

'Mister General,' said Baby, tugging at his jacket, 'Lunch is served. Come on, we've made you something to eat.' She gestured towards the rest of us.

The General turned around and we all nodded. Baby kept pulling him by the arm with her dirty hands. He followed her wearily with a smile on his face.

'We've made lunch for you,' said Pasquetta.

'Thank you,' said the General. 'You're very kind.'

We took the General to a clearing in the woods where there were some large rocks to sit on. On the other stones sat Fifi, the doll, Tro-tro, the yellow bear, then Pierino, Pasquetta, and Zeffirino. Lea and I tended to the General. We sat him down and began to serve him lunch. Baby put a napkin around his neck.

'Have some soup, Mister General,' said Lea, red in the face and with tears in her eyes from having to constantly blow on the fire to stop it from going out.

The General drank from the chipped mug and said, 'Very nice.'

'Would you like some more?' I asked.

'No, thank you, I'm fine,' said the General.

'Now for dessert. We have some crushed chestnuts with pinecones and wine.'

The general drank from the glass and ate off the laurel leaves.

'Are you enjoying yourself?' asked Baby, fanning him with a dry palm leaf.

'Yes, very much so,' said the General.

But Hainz ruined it all when he arrived, snapping to attention and shouting something in German. He took the General away, but not before he'd thanked us and filled his pockets with the pebbles and shiny stones that we'd given him.

(25)

The Villa was surrounded by machine guns and ammunition. Apologising for the inconvenience, the General sent word through his assistant that he would need another room. Hainz did a military salute and then went to tell Uncle.

We were all sitting at the table, which had been perfectly laid by the servants who were now circling us with their trays. Despite the war and the General's slow takeover of the whole Villa, our lives went on in much the same fashion. If the food was overcooked, if there were no fresh flowers on the table, if the glasses that had been brought out weren't from the crystal set, if the floors weren't shining, if Rosa hadn't ironed her white pinafore and wasn't wearing her bonnet, or if Cosimo had lost a button on his livery, Uncle would get angry. The huge crystal chandelier above the dinner table shone its light on us just as it always had.

'Do you always wash your neck?' I asked the General's aide the following morning as he leaned over the fountain in the garden.

'Yes, every morning,' he said.

'I don't. Is it dirty?' I asked with the little German I had picked up from Aunt Katchen.

'No, it's clean.'

'What's your name?'

'Hainz.'

'Mine's Penny. I have to wash my doll's clothes. Her name is Doll. I need to use the water fountain. Does it take you long to wash your neck?'

'No.'

'You've been washing it for half an hour.'

Hainz laughed and began to wash Doll's clothes.

That night I heard a voice under the window calling my name. It was a soldier. I looked out and saw it was Hainz. He brought an ocarina up to his mouth and began to play *Lili Marleen*. I had promised Hainz a big piece of cake if he helped me wash Doll's dress. I put on my slippers so I wouldn't make any noise.

'Come on,' I told Hainz. 'Be quiet.'

I was worried Uncle would catch me. But Hainz was so kind and his blue eyes lit up with joy. I took a piece of cake out of the cupboard and gave it to him. He sat down and looked at me. I poured him some wine. Hainz finished the whole bottle. I put it back. Then I brushed the crumbs off the marble table. I climbed onto his lap and started pulling whatever I could find out of his breast pocket. There were some photographs: Hainz's mother and father.

'You want some jam?'

'*Jawohl.*'

Hainz finished the whole jar.

'Now go away,' I said.

Hainz squeezed me tight and kissed me on the forehead. As he squeezed me, the buttons on his uniform dug into me, and his beard, which was badly shaven, made my cheeks red.

'See you tomorrow,' I said, pushing him out of the door.

THE SKY IS FALLING

'*Ja,*' he said, smiling. He lifted me up off the floor and squeezed me again. Then he put me back down.

When I crawled back into bed, Baby asked me where I had been.

'I was giving Hainz dessert.'

I could hear the refrain of *Rosamunda* floating up from the courtyard. Through the window came the sound of Hainz's ocarina accompanied by the song of grasshoppers. He played for a long time until I fell asleep.

I loved Hainz just like I loved Lieutenant Friedrich and Leonardo and I thought that when I was older I would like to have many husbands.

(26)

As soon as I woke up, I thought about how entertaining it was to have the Villa so full of new faces and guests. And I thought about Hainz and the General who'd been working through the night. I could hear the sound of Hainz's boots as he paced up and down and stood to attention.

Baby and I kept finding excuses to go past the General's room. One day we were so desperate to see him that we turned up with a mop and broom and said we had been sent to do the cleaning. I began to dust the papers on the General's desk, while Baby dusted some crates on the floor.

'Don't touch!' the General told her, '*Boom!*'

'Boom?' Baby asked.

'Boom, boom,' said the General.

'Boom!' said Hainz, pointing at the crates.

'Boom,' Baby repeated and started to dust the General's coat, which was hanging on the chair.

'I have a daughter just like her,' said the General, gesturing to Baby.

'I brought you these,' Baby said, pointing at the daisies on his table.

But Uncle forbade us to go into the Eastern Wing of the Villa and the Western Wing too, which was where the soldiers slept.

It was hot and the cicadas were so loud that sometimes I liked to cover my ears with my hands to remind myself what silence sounded like.

Hainz entered the dining room while Rosa was serving breakfast. The General sent word to Uncle that he would very much like to play a game of chess but that he had no one to play with. Uncle replied that he was 'at the General's command,' and then Hainz saluted again, snapping his heels together and bowing before leaving the room.

'I wonder why they have to make all that noise with their boots just to say a couple words!'

Rosa began to laugh so hard that she couldn't pour Uncle's coffee and he scolded her for it. Suddenly we all felt scared because Uncle wasn't laughing at all. He looked very serious.

'Let's go before Uncle scolds us too.'

Uncle frowned when I stood up and accidentally knocked a plate off the table.

'Penny, you will go and write *I will not break plates at dinner* one hundred times in your punishment journal.'

This kind of punishment was the worst of all, because it would take me a whole day to write out a hundred sentences like that.

The General arrived, preceded by Hainz, who was carrying the chess board. He knocked on the door to Uncle's study. We could barely contain ourselves as we spied on what was going on. Was Uncle really going to play chess with the General? We watched the scene unfold through the keyhole. Hainz left, but not before standing to attention two or three times. The General entered and Uncle gestured for him to sit down. They took up their seats facing each other and Uncle pointed at the chess board. They stayed in silence like this for nearly half an hour, slowly moving pieces across the board.

After a gruelling wait behind the door, we saw that Hainz was coming back. He knocked, entered the room, and said something in German. The General got up and followed Hainz out, half bowing to Uncle. They abandoned the game halfway through. The General bumped into Katchen as she was coming in and kissed her hand.

'Can I finish the game?' I asked. 'Let me see what I'd do if I were the General.'

'Let's see,' said Uncle, amused.

'I'd capture your knight!'

'Very nice, and I'd capture your king,' Uncle said.

(27)

Marie had long since abandoned her bicycle in favour of horse riding. She had started wearing trousers like a tomboy, running around in the fields and coming back to the Villa all flushed, having left the job of bringing Italo back to the stables to the farmer. Sometimes Baby and I were allowed to trot up and down the avenue on Lola. They'd usually stick us both on the same saddle.

One day, Marie came back saying that the soldiers had taken Cencetti's oxen. Uncle sent word to the General that he should give back the oxen to Cencetti, that it wasn't *just* to take them from him.

The General ordered his men to give back the oxen.

Uncle sent word that it wasn't *just* that someone had taken his favourite fountain pen. Uncle also sent word to the General that it wasn't *just* when the soldiers went through our wardrobes and took things that did not belong to them. The General gave the order that the army shouldn't touch anything that wasn't theirs.

Since it was Sunday, there was Mass at the Villa's chapel. Baby and I snuck into the sacristy to say hello to the priest, who asked us if we'd been praying for Uncle's soul. I said yes. But he said that this wasn't enough anymore because not only was Uncle's soul in danger but his body too. Uncle was in danger, the priest said, because the Germans had decided to take all the Jews off to prison.

That's what the priest said. Since Uncle didn't believe in Jesus, the priest said, the Germans wanted to take him to prison.

The priest said that Uncle should run away and hide because otherwise the Germans would take him away and that to stay was pure madness. But I found it hard to believe that Hainz or the General would want to harm Uncle.

The priest was so worried that he requested a meeting with Uncle several times. This was strange because Uncle and the priest hadn't exchanged a word since the time Uncle had refused to send us to Mass.

Uncle received the priest and we watched them through the keyhole. Every time he visited, the priest left looking defeated because Uncle didn't want to run away. He'd speak to Uncle for a long time to try to convince him. He would say, 'You are in danger, you must flee, it's madness to stay.' But Uncle would shake his head and repeat the same sentence every time: 'I've done nothing wrong, I've never hurt anyone, why should I flee? I have nothing to fear. Why should I hide? Isn't that right, Katchen?' and he'd look to Aunty, who would just about manage to nod, saying, 'Yes, darling,' as tears streamed down her face.

The priest came to the Villa a third and final time. When he left, he told Pippone that Uncle was crazy and repeated that the two of us should pray for him.

Even Pippone came to the Villa to offer Uncle refuge in his house in the woods, but Uncle kept on insisting that he had nothing to hide and nothing to fear. At that very moment, and to Pippone's great amazement, the General and Hainz came in carrying the chess board to play with Uncle.

Uncle was right. Uncle always told the truth. He was Truth and Justice personified and so he couldn't be wrong.

I examined the face of the German general as he played chess with Uncle. I wanted to look deep into his eyes. But his eyes were so clear and blue that I wasn't able to see anything but goodness.

'Are you good?' asked Baby, looking him in the eyes.

Uncle sent us to play in the garden. But I was scared. At night, whenever I heard cars pull up to the

Villa, I'd leap out of bed with my heart going *boom boom* in my chest, terrified that they were coming for Uncle. I'd tiptoe out of my room and look down the great staircase at the officers coming and going, saluting one another by snapping their heels and shouting orders.

I was scared. I wasn't sure why. I knew full well that Uncle was right and so was Aunt Katchen, and that the General was good. But I was still scared. What if Uncle's truth was not true? What was the truth? I wished the truth would appear in big letters in the sky. While Uncle, Aunt, Annie, Baby, Marie, Rosa, Cosimo, and Elsa were sleeping, the Germans were hard at work. Were they plotting against Uncle? I was scared. I heard boots approaching.

It was Hainz.

'Hainz!' I threw my arms around his neck. 'Hainz, do you love us?'

'*Ja, ja, jawohl.*'

'All of us? Annie, Marie and Uncle too?'

Hainz led me back up to my bedroom and said good night.

'Does the General love Uncle too?'

'*Ja, ja, gute Nacht.*'

Hainz left, gently shutting the door. But I was still scared. The wind blew and the curtains swelled, waving like ghosts.

(28)

More soldiers had arrived at the Villa and there were more cannons and ammunition in the courtyard too.

'Don't you ever fire them?' I said to a soldier.

We could see more cannons being moved up the road that led north.

'Why don't you show us?' asked Baby, touching a machine gun.

It was quite irritating to have all these cannons lying around and never see them fired. All we heard was the roar of the enemy's cannons, which had become a background noise as unceasing as that of the cicadas.

It was lunchtime and Elsa called us inside. Marie showed up to the table in her Sunday dress, wearing heels and lipstick. At first this had been a novelty for everyone.

Since the soldiers had arrived, Marie had taken to wearing her Sunday best and heels, and putting on a lot of airs. She had begun to style her hair and had started putting on lipstick.

'What are you doing with your hips?'

She was swinging her hips like Rosa.

'Shut up, silly, I've always walked like this,' she replied.

'Sure, sure...' said Baby, beginning to swing her hips.

'You two really are unbearable!' said Marie, angrily tossing anything she could find at us. That stupid Marie didn't even realise how much it hurt when she threw a hairbrush at my head like that.

Annie also started swinging her hips, and later, just as we were about to go to bed, she took off almost all her clothes and did the dance of the Shulamite. She made Baby and me clap our hands and then she got carried away with the rhythm, spinning around in front of the mirror.

'Don't you think I'm beautiful too?' asked Annie, and she started whirling again. 'Don't you think I'm beautiful too?' she repeated, resentfully.

The following morning, we went into the woods to pinch the heads off the cicadas and put them in a little matchbox. We kept the bodies in another box and the wings in a third. Then we returned to the Villa and I went into the salon, and what did I see there but Marie and Lieutenant Friedrich kissing!

What would Uncle say? More importantly, what would Leonardo say? I had slipped behind the velvet curtain that hung beneath the big picture in order to get a better look at the two of them. Marie was leaning against the piano and he came closer and then... he kissed her again!

I ran away. I was sad. I wanted to marry Marie. One day I'd said to her, 'Marie, please don't shout at me, I love you. If I were a man I'd marry you!' She'd watched me with her mouth hanging open. Now I was sad that a man had come to take her soul. What about me? Would Marie have enough space in her heart for us children now the Lieutenant was in there?

'Would you marry me if you were a man?' I said to Marie, later that day. Marie laughed and didn't answer me. So I made the same proposal to Baby, who replied with a firm yes, planting a jam-smeared kiss on my cheek.

What a shame grown-up girls were like that, ready to forget us as soon as the first Lieutenant came along.

We were watching the General and Uncle play chess. Today, the General asked Uncle if he was a Jew. Uncle said yes.

I was afraid because I no longer knew what the truth was. I looked to Uncle but Uncle was smiling.

At lunch, Uncle smiled at Aunt Katchen, whose eyes were red, and placed his hand on her shoulder.

'Dear, please go check if lunch has been served.'

Aunt Katchen went to the kitchen, and a little while later Cosimo came out and rang the gong.

Annie and Baby rushed in from the garden to the table, and Marie left her red jumper behind on the chair and came too.

Uncle scolded Cosimo because a gold button was missing from his jacket, and because his white gloves weren't perfectly white. He scolded Elsa because lunch was late and the rice was overcooked, and then he scolded Rosa because the floors weren't sparkling clean.

But when Uncle smiled, all my fears flew away.

In the evening, at dinner, Uncle was still smiling as the English bombarded the Villa. We were all scared, even Cosimo: his hands were shaking as he held the tray and he kept saying that the planes 'had it in for us'. But Uncle said no, that Cosimo was talking nonsense and the planes were headed for Florence. Meanwhile, the whole Villa shook, and the glass chandelier jingled.

Marie and Annie and Baby's faces were white with fear, and Aunt Katchen was looking pleadingly at Uncle, begging him to let us go down to the cellar or the oil mill. Uncle pointed out that downstairs was full of soldiers and peasants.

Uncle smiled as if nothing was wrong, and even tried to be funny, which he only ever did at Christmas or on our birthdays.

Hainz came in shouting and went to close all the windows, saying that the English had seen light coming from the Villa, and now they were targeting it. The Germans were running up and down the stairs, adding to the confusion with their cries.

I held my breath as a plane dropped low, just above our heads.

We heard a machine gun and then a great big noise, like the end of the world.

'Bring in the dessert,' said Uncle to Cosimo, and Cosimo served us all dessert, and then the aeroplanes were gone.

(30)

Baby crawled into my bed. I heard her approach, her bare feet on the tiles, then her weight was on me and her voice in my ear.

'We forgot to say our prayers for Uncle!'

'I'm doing a special penance for Uncle.'

'What are you doing?'

'I'm holding my arms open like Jesus on the cross in order to suffer like him.'

'How long will you stay like that?'

'I have to count to a thousand.'

'Let me do it too.'

'But you can't count.'

'I can.'

'Yes, but you have to do it on the ground, like Saint Barnabas.'

That night I dreamt about Jesus. Jesus was being whipped by the soldiers. But when he saw me, he smiled like he did in my book where Jesus was smiling at the children.

'You know,' I told him, 'I'm going to go and see Pilate now to tell him not to let them crucify you.' Jesus smiled and said it was too late. So I went to Pilate and I said to him, 'Can't you see they are about to kill Jesus, our Lord?' But he just kept on washing his hands.

I was all set to tell Pilate he was an ugly toad.

'No,' said Jesus, 'You mustn't tell him that.'

But I went back to see Pilate anyway, who was dressed all in green, and I told him exactly what I had wanted to say, and I even made faces at him, but he just kept washing his hands. I began to scream, but the soldiers had already come for Jesus.

'No! No! You can't kill our Lord Jesus!''

I clung to their clothing as they carried him away.

God the Father was looking down from above, doing nothing to help Jesus.

'They're about to murder Jesus, the son of God!'

The angels were flying up and down, singing Hosanna with lilies in their hands. Jesus was alone in the olive grove.

'Why isn't anyone doing anything?'

Three angels came down disguised as three gentlemen. Maybe they would do something. The Devil was advancing on tiptoe. The soldiers were pacing up and down, making a big noise with their boots. Jesus Christ was alone in the olive grove, crying.

'Can't you see Christ is crying?' I said, hurrying to join him.

'Can you tell me how to get to the olive grove?'

I went to Jesus and I said, 'I want to die for you.'

'Thanks,' said Jesus, 'But now leave me alone, I need to have a word with Satan.'

I went to find Satan, and I said, 'Jesus wants to speak to you.'

He was swatting off flies with his tail. The sky was all black, without a single star, and everything was as calm as if nothing was happening; people were idling in the middle of the road.

'Can't you see that the son of God is about to die?'

And I ran to get help.

I ran into Baby, 'They're going to kill Jesus. Where is the olive grove? Where are the Apostles?'

'I don't know,' said Baby.

'Excuse me, sir,' I said to a passing man, who turned out to be the custodian at our school, 'They're about to crucify Jesus.'

'Yes,' he said, 'I'm on my way to watch. Everyone's going!'

'But it can't happen! He mustn't die!'

So I went to Jesus and I said to him, 'Come with me and Baby, there's a hiding place in the woods.'

But Jesus told us to go and get him his best Sunday clothes. So I went to the Villa and looked in Uncle's wardrobe, through all his clothes, and finally managed to find his white suit and his wide-brimmed hat, but then I saw Jesus arrive escorted by the soldiers, and Pilate was there too, still dressed in green.

'Let me through!' I said, 'I'm bringing Jesus his suit.'

'No,' he said, 'you always tell lies.'

Then Pasquetta began to sing *Salve Regina* and everyone else joined in, even Pilate, and I looked up at the cross and saw that Jesus had Uncle's face.

(31)

I couldn't fall asleep again. I tried to wake Baby and Annie, but they kept sleeping. I went to Marie and managed to wake her up. I told her I'd had a bad dream and that Uncle had been in it and that I was scared. But she began to comfort me the way grown-up girls do when they want to play Mother.

'We have to do something,' I said to Marie, but she said it had only been a bad dream and that it was over now. She turned on her lamp and explained that I probably just had indigestion and sent me back to bed.

But I was still scared. Was it possible that I was the only one who was scared? Everyone else was asleep. Couldn't they feel the danger looming over the Villa like a great monster?

I could feel this danger, but it had no face. I could feel this enemy, but it had no voice. It was sitting in ambush somewhere inside the Villa, somewhere near my bed. I could hear it breathing, but I couldn't see it. I tiptoed over to the window and looked through the sheer curtains.

It was hot. The moon was so round it frightened me. From up there, the moon could see the monster crouching on top of the house. I didn't dare lean out of the window for fear I might catch a glimpse of its tail.

Lorenza Mazzetti

I was scared. My hands were scared, my heart was scared, every strand of hair on my head was scared.

Why was nobody answering me? Why was nobody listening to me?

With my heart stuffed in my mouth, I tiptoed into Uncle's bedroom.

'What is it?' Uncle asked.

And Aunt Katchen asked, 'Do you feel ill, Penny?'

'I'm scared!'

I burst into tears, repeating that I was scared.

'What are you scared of?' Uncle asked.

All of a sudden I didn't know what to say. I repeated, 'I'm scared,' and continued to stammer.

Aunt Katchen thought I had a tummy ache, so she sat me down in the armchair and went downstairs to make me a cup of chamomile tea.

Uncle put on his blue robe and asked me if my stomach was hurting.

I said I was scared because he didn't believe in God or Baby Jesus and that his life and his soul were in danger. But Uncle didn't seem to understand me, and because I was still so distressed he took me on his lap and I told him then that the Germans were going to take him away and put him in a camp together with all the others who weren't Christian and that the priest had told me so.

He started talking in a grave voice and said he believed in something called human dignity, but I didn't fully understand what that meant and so I repeated my question, 'Why don't you believe in Jesus?'

When he saw me crying so hard, Uncle got up and said all right, from now on he would believe in the Baby Jesus.

'And in the Resurrection of the Body too?' I asked.
'In the Resurrection too.'
'And in our beloved Madonnina?'
'Yes.'
'But do you really believe it? All of it?' I insisted.
At that point, Baby came in looking for me, not having found me in bed.
I was saying, 'Will you believe in the Holy Spirit?'
'In the Holy Spirit,' Uncle repeated.
'And in the Holy Catholic Church.'
'In the Holy Catholic Church.'
'And in the communion of saints?'
'Yes, in the communion of saints too.'
'And in eternal life?' Baby added.
'Yes, Baby, I will believe in eternal life too. And it is precisely for that reason that we don't have anything to fear, isn't that right? But we'll talk more tomorrow and you can tell me about Jesus then. Now go to bed.'
Baby had climbed onto Uncle as if he were a tree.

(32)

Today I woke up to an empty Villa. The General and his soldiers, Hainz and Lieutenant Friedrich, had left to travel north with all of their cannons.

Before leaving, the General kissed Aunt Katchen's hand and asked if he could be of help in taking any of her correspondence up north, since the postal service was no longer working.

I filled Hainz's pockets with the white bread he liked so much.

Lorenza Mazzetti

As the General's camouflaged car drove off my eyes filled with tears, and I felt as if a great void had been left in the Villa.

Later that day, Uncle played with us little ones because it was Baby's birthday. On this day everything was allowed because it was Baby's day. In a few months it would be my birthday, and then I'd also get to ask Uncle to grant me a wish.

Baby's wish was for Uncle to play with us, and so for one day there were no grown-ups at the Villa, only children. We played *mosca cieca* in the garden. Uncle let us blindfold his eyes. He came looking for us in his big white hat. We tugged on his jacket and laughed. Uncle was so funny. He couldn't see us and so he couldn't catch us. Oh, but now he had Baby!

We switched games. We played hopscotch. Uncle stepped on the line and lost the game. We all started to laugh. Even Annie and Marie. Today everyone had to play with us.

Uncle played Queen's Footsteps with us. First we sang a *conta* to decide who would be the queen. Baby was the queen. She had to slowly count to three and then suddenly turn around. While she had her back to us, we had to get as close as we could to her, until we could touch her. Whoever touched her first became the queen, but if we were caught while we were still moving, we had to go back to the starting line.

'One, two, three...!'

Baby spun around. We were all motionless and we'd all got one step closer to her. Even Uncle.

'One, two, three...!'

Baby turned again. Uncle had taken a huge step, he had almost reached her, but alas, Uncle lost his balance! He was still moving!

'I saw you move!' Baby screamed, 'You have to go back!

'That's not true, I wasn't moving!' Uncle protested.

'It's true, it's true, I saw you!'

Uncle went back to where he'd started, which made Baby explode with delight.

Next we played hide and seek.

Uncle was so funny! He advanced cautiously, looking for but never finding us, while we could spot him hiding in the bushes in an instant because of his big white hat.

'Found you!' I screamed in his ears.

Ah, what a beautiful day! How I wished all days could be like this.

Though people always said there was no replacing one's real mother and father, I couldn't imagine how I could ever have loved my own mother more than Aunt Katchen or my father more than Uncle.

Aunt Katchen had given Baby a doll she'd made from some of her old clothes, and she'd told Baby it was her rag mamma. Later that afternoon, we walked back to the creek because Baby had left her rag mamma behind. I tried to track her down by smelling the air. Aunt Katchen's perfume was very distinctive and since she had made the doll using her old clothes, the doll smelled of her. When we couldn't find it, I told Baby she could have my doll instead.

'No, I don't want her because she's your mamma.'

'But if she's my mamma, then she's your mamma too!'

'That's not true,' Baby said, and she began to cry. Aunt Katchen couldn't find any more old clothes to cut up, so she had to make Baby a new doll from her light blue nightdress.

Baby wandered across the lawn with her new rag mamma under her arm, kissing her and talking to her, telling her about this and that. She would walk through the fields with the doll in her arms, sometimes pausing to pick a daisy to offer her as a gift. Her rag mamma's long sky blue train fluttered in the evening breeze.

I watched her stroll along the grass for a long time. I was very upset to see that she had forgotten me, and that now all her love and her kisses were for another girl.

I sadly hoisted myself up on the medlar tree, wearing a long face.

(33)

'The Madonna ate everything!' cried Pasquetta.

She hurtled towards us barefoot and panting, somehow managing not to hurt herself. Behind her were Pierino and Zeffirino.

'It's true! The Madonna has eaten everything!' they shouted.

Maybe the Madonna was hungry?

'Come and see!'

The Madonna had come down from the sky and accepted our gifts, taking them back up with her. We stopped to look at the little statue of the Madonna that tasted like sugar. Baby asked why the Madonna kept her foot on the snake.

'She's killing the Devil,' said Lea.

The Madonna was so beautiful, dressed in heavenly blue!

'Maybe your ma's up there with her.'

'Do you think so?' Baby asked.

'Together with the Holy Spirit.'

I looked at the holy card of Jesus, who was holding a heart surrounded by thorns in his hands. That heart must have been carrying all the pain of the world.

I looked at Jesus's face. How handsome he was with his blonde hair and beard! I didn't understand God very well, but I understood Jesus: I loved him, and I was sorry I'd missed his coming on Earth.

'Is God the Father also with Mamma?'

On the holy card there was also a little white lamb.

'That little lamb is Jesus too,' said Pierino.

There was another holy card featuring a little girl who'd just taken her first communion and behind her was the angel Gabriel, who looked a little like Jesus, only without the beard.

'Every single one of us has the angel Gabriel behind us.'

Immediately I felt the presence of the angel Gabriel behind me, and I knew that he was just like me, except for the wings.

'And what's the dove on his head?' asked Baby.

'That's the Holy Spirit.'

The Holy Spirit was the third person in the Holy Trinity, Baby the fourth, I the fifth, Pierino the sixth, Lea the seventh, and Zeffirino the eighth person of the Trinity.

I told Annie that the Madonna had eaten everything. She didn't believe me. So I told her that if she didn't believe me she should come and see for herself, but that she shouldn't tell anyone else. I asked Pasquetta and the others if Annie could come to one of our Masses. They said yes, as long as she said confession first.

So Annie came to say confession. She couldn't stop confessing. How many sins she had!

'You forgot about that time you put salt in our soup,' said Baby.

'Yes.'

'And when you put a lizard in our bed.'

'Yes, and also when I ate all your chocolate,' Annie said contritely.

'Ah, it was you!'

Pierino condemned her to ten lashes on her bum.

'Stop! Stop!' said Annie

'Will you also pray for Uncle's soul?' I asked and explained that Uncle was in danger.

'Yes,' said Annie.

'And for our Duce?'

'Yes, for the Duce too.'

'Get on your knees.'

Annie kneeled, and we did too, and we all prayed. We had put pebbles under our knees so we would suffer more.

(34)

I thought I'd heard a rustling sound. All of a sudden, a white hare leapt out of the undergrowth. But she ran away as soon as she saw us.

'It's the Madonna!' said Lea.

We looked on, dumbstruck.

We hid in the bushes to watch the Holy Spirit as he descended upon the Cross. He appeared as a sparrow, and after he had pecked up some biscuit crumbs, he flew back up to Heaven on the head of John the Baptist and landed in the hands of God. From there he flew to perch on the head of Jesus, who sat to the right of our Almighty Father.

One day the Devil came in the guise of a rooster. He scared off the sparrow and polished off what was left of the food. You could tell he was the Devil by his evil expression.

'We must kill the Devil.'

The rooster was still there, and I thought I caught a glimpse of evil in his eyes. I was afraid that the Devil would take possession of my body and soul.

With a scream, Pierino leaped on the Devil, but the Devil slipped out of his hands. Pasquetta jumped on the Devil, who did not want to die. We all set upon him with sticks and stones, beating him. Lea struck the Devil's neck so many times that his head came off. We left him at the foot of the Cross and began to pray.

Then Pierino turned to us and said that Satan wasn't dead yet. He'd leapt up to Heaven and was clinging onto its edge and so when he plummeted back down to earth he would take a piece of the sky with him.

'Really?' said Annie.

We all raised our hands to hold the sky up. Lea began to sing. Our arms were raised, our faces burning with the effort of holding the sky in place. The sky was about to fall, the sky was falling; we were standing with our arms raised to hold up the sky. Satan was about to fall down into Hell, where his name would be Lucifer. And yet there we were, our arms raised up to the falling sky. We were red from the effort. Would anyone help us?

Satan was about to fall, behold now he falls, the angel Gabriel looking down from above with his flaming sword, and all the angels singing *Hosanna, Hosanna.*

(35)

Tosca, the peasant girl who helped with the washing at the Villa, had fallen ill.

'Tosca is not well, she's got evil spirits in her.'

'What are you talking about?'

'Yeah, yeah, she don't eat no food no more, all she wants is coal and ash!'

Pierino said that Tosca had spirits in her body because somebody had cast a spell on her.

'An old woman did it, and every time she wants to eat she can't because the Old Lady appears, shaking her head.'

'And where is the Old Lady?'

'Only Tosca can see her, and when she does she starts screaming'

'If the Old Lady keeps shaking her head, Tosca will die.'

We went to see Tosca.

'She's sick,' they told us and wouldn't let us in. At dusk the women came with their black veils to say the rosary.

One morning we were waiting for Tosca's parents, Evelina and Pietrone, to leave the house so we could go upstairs to see her.

Crouched behind the bushes like that, I felt very close to the earth and the ants.

'Look! Ants! That one's carrying a piece of wheat!'

'That isn't wheat,' said Lea, crushing the ants one by one.

'You're hurting them,' said Baby.

'Ants don't feel pain,' said Lea, continuing to crush them one by one.

'We're so big they can't see us.'

'Imagine if a giant stood over us and crushed us with his thumb.'

'There are no giants in Heaven, only God.'

'Well then, imagine if God crushed us with his thumb.'

'He might crush you but not me,' said Lea, as she continued to crush ants.

'God doesn't have thumbs.'

'God doesn't, but the giants in Heaven do.'

'God is in Heaven, you moron.'

'Stinky!' said Baby to Lea, sticking her tongue out.

'Oi, do I stink?' Lea asked, coming closer so I could smell her.

'No, you don't stink.' I said.

'Yes, you do!' said Baby.

'No, I don't stink. Here, Penny, smell me. Do I stink?'

'No, you don't stink.'

'Yes, yes, you always stink like a barn,' said Baby.

'That's a smell, Baby, not a stink. Lea is right about that.'

We smelled each other. My dress was white with big dark red polka dots. Baby's dress was pink with little blue flowers. It was slightly transparent and you could see her embroidered petticoat underneath. The ribbon on my head was white and Baby's was pink.

Lorenza Mazzetti

I wondered why the Old Lady wanted to hurt Tosca. Tosca, who was so beautiful with her red cheeks, who was always singing, had been in bed for a fortnight with the Old Lady sitting next to her and shaking her head.

'Tosca! Tosca!' I whispered in her ear, when we finally made it into the house.

'Tosca! Tosca! Tosca!' said Baby, standing on her tiptoes next to the big white bed.

'Tosca, can you hear us?'

'Here,' said Pierino, placing a small handful of blackberries on her lips. But Tosca didn't hear us and stared straight up at the wooden beams of the ceiling. Pierino's blackberries fell onto the pillow, staining it black.

'Bring me the coals,' said Tosca. She seemed to be speaking to someone.

'She's speaking to the Old Lady.'

'Tosca!' Baby shouted, standing even higher on her tiptoes and leaning on the big bed.

The bed was large, high, and made of painted iron. On the white wall above it there was the Madonna, ascending to Heaven; small men were gathered inside her mantle, gazing upwards to the sky. At one point Tosca began to scream as if she were having a fit, biting the bed sheets as if she were fighting somebody.

Terrified, we ran down the narrow stairs and out in the fields.

*

The sorcerer had said to Tosca's sister, Ginetta, that she must kill a rooster and take out its heart, then go and find a toad and get somebody to pee on it.

Beppe was an old man who wanted to make love to Tosca, and whom Tosca had rejected because she was already making love to Brunetto. That was why Beppe had put a spell on her.

For Tosca to be cured, twenty pins had to be driven into the rooster's heart. Ginetta, who was as beautiful as Tosca, had to bring all these things to the sorcerer by moonlight, and she asked the rest of us, Zeffirino and Pierino, to bring her a toad. Ginetta was crying. She took out a rosary with white beads for the *Pater Noster* and black for *Ora Patris* and said she would give it to Zeffirino in return for the favour.

I had a rosary, too. I always said two *Hail Marys* and two *Pater Nosters* for all my relatives and friends, for Mamma and Papà who were in Heaven, and for all the people I saw on the street whom I hadn't met yet, though I often fell asleep before I reached the end. I always prayed for the Duce and the Fatherland too, and for all the Italian soldiers so that they wouldn't lose even a single battle, and so that the English would never make it to where we were.

I'd made my own rosary out of medlar pits. I wanted to become a saint.

Zeffirino came back with a toad.

'Did you see the Old Lady?'

Zeffirino said he'd met the Old Lady in the woods and that she had the smallest eyes he'd ever seen.

'So I looked at her, and my eyes went big like this... and then small like this... but she just stood there staring at me and it looked like she was shaking her head, *no no no...*'

Ginetta was waiting for us at the crossroads, sitting under a tree. She'd probably thought we weren't coming back.

'Here it is,' Zeffirino held up the toad. 'Here's your toad.'

Ginetta took it and gave us the rosary in return. She started up the hill, alone. She was going to see the sorcerer.

*

The following day as we were sitting down to eat, Elsa came in and asked Uncle if he would speak to Pippone, who was in the kitchen in tears. Uncle called him in.

'Master,' Pippone said, shuffling awkwardly into the dining room and taking off his hat. He was sliding around on the polished floor.

'Master, if you could help us...' he kept twisting his hat in his hands and bending over to wipe up the dust that had fallen from his clothes onto the floor with his handkerchief.

'She's dying is our Tosca. If only your Master could bring over the priest with the car, before it's too late...'

Uncle sent Cosimo to pick up the priest in the car. Cosimo returned with the priest all dressed up as if for Mass, with his white lace and incense and holy water and a hat on his head. He had even brought along an altar boy.

Cosimo told us afterwards that Tosca had started shrieking like crazy when she saw the priest, throwing anything she could find at him.

'She must have really been possessed to throw all that stuff at the priest!' said Pasquetta.

Cosimo said that four of them had had to hold Tosca down because she'd been writhing and bashing

THE SKY IS FALLING   147

her head and legs against the bed. The priest had put a crucifix on her chest while the others held her down, and the spirits had left through her mouth, hissing and screaming as they escaped through the window. We'd been waiting in the car at the bottom of the hill, listening.

The priest had blessed Tosca, and once all the devils had left through her mouth, she'd stopped screaming. I was a little worried that all those devils that had come out of Tosca's mouth might get into mine or Baby's or Pasquetta's, or worst of all into Uncle's.

The priest started to walk down the hill towards the car, stumbling in his black robe.

'I've never gone to confession,' said Baby.

'Who knows how many sins you have committed,' said the altar boy. 'Who knows how many...'

'I've never said confession either,' I interrupted.

'So many sins,' said the altar boy. He said his soul was whiter than white because he'd gone to confession that morning and so all his sins had been washed away. How I wished I could wash my soul in the same way as you washed your ears or your neck in the morning and feel white all over with Jesus inside my body!

Our chauffeur was waiting silently in the car. He almost never spoke to us. He intimidated Baby and me. The parish priest blessed Ginetta, who disappeared back into the house, and then he came towards us, holding his crucifix in one hand and the hat which the wind had blown off his head in the other.

The priest said nothing. He climbed into the car and began to read the breviary.

36

The roar of the cannons had become so monotonous that even the birds were no longer frightened enough to bother leaving their trees.

'Shall we play Adam and Eve?'

'Who's going to be the Devil?'

'Not me.'

Pierino said we should do a *conta* to see who would play the devil, and he did it by singing a song that went like this: 'One two three for the king and the queen, *nanana-na-na*...' and so on.

Pasquetta was 'it'.

'I don't wanna play the Devil.'

'You got to, though.'

'You spoiled the count.'

'Pierino always cheats. He changes the song every time and points at whoever he wants.'

'God's sake, I ain't playing the Devil.'

'That's not true, it's how the count goes,' he repeated the song, pointing his finger at Pasquetta again.

'I said I'm not playing the Devil.'

'Sure as hell you'll never be a saint with that face!' said Lea.

Pasquetta was about to jump on Lea, but then she remembered that she'd taken communion and now she had Jesus inside her.

'Are we playing or what?'

'We don't have an apple.'

'Baby can go and get one.'

Baby hid her face in her floral dress, pulling its skirt up like a tent. She stood like that with her dress over her head, thinking we couldn't see her. She was looking at us through the fabric.

'Come on, Baby, we're playing Adam and Eve. You have to sing. I'm the angel Gabriel.'

'No,' said Baby with her dress pulled over her head.

'Leave birdbrain alone!'

'Baby's always wasting our time. She'll never be a saint.'

Baby uncovered her head and made faces at us.

'I'm tired of playing the Devil,' said Pasquetta, perched in the tree, 'if you don't come right away, I'm leaving.' And she left. So Zeffirino put on the Devil's mincing little voice and offered me the apple, saying, 'Penny, do you want this apple?'

'Go away, ugly Devil, don't tempt me.'

The Devil turned to Pierino instead and said, 'Pierino, do you want this apple?'

'Go away, ugly Devil, don't lead me into temptation.'

And so on and so forth.

'Baby, Baby, eat the apple,' said Zeffirino in the Devil's voice, and to try and tempt her he took a little bite himself.

'Get away, ugly Devil!'

'It's so good!' said Zeffirino, chewing with his mouth open and coming closer to her.

'But you're eating it all!'

Zeffirino stopped, looking cross.

'Am I the Devil or what? I'm done playing. I'll never be a saint now for playing the Devil.'

'Out!' shouted the angel with the whip, 'Get out of the Garden of Eden!'

We let ourselves be whipped for a long time because it was only through suffering that others could be redeemed of their sins.

37

The cannon's roar had become even louder. Baby and I climbed up the tree every day to watch the distant columns of soldiers heading north along the main road. They looked like a colony of black ants.

Every day new German battalions passed through the Villa, occupying the barns and rooms of the house only to leave the following day. We could hear the cries of the pigs and the calves as the soldiers carried them off and cut their throats in the courtyard. Hearing the animals cry made Annie burst into tears, so I hugged her and tried to comfort her.

We dragged her down to the creek where she wouldn't be able to hear them.

'Annie, don't cry.'

'I'm scared,' said Annie, sobbing. 'They sound like people screaming.'

'Don't say that,' said Baby.

For a moment, I imagined the blood of the calves flooding through the corridors of the house and submerging the Villa.

'Annie, please don't cry.'

She plugged her ears with her fingers. How could I ever have hated Annie?

'Annie, I love you, do you know that?'

Then Baby fell in the stream that ran under Pietro's house, where it was thick with elms and bamboo canes.

I went to tell Marie that Baby had fallen into the water and hurt herself. Elsa changed Baby's clothes, shouting that we were bad girls and that she was always having to clean us up, that the Master wanted us to be tidy and clean at all times but that we liked getting dirty on purpose.

Not too long before, in fact, Baby had gone round to Zeffirino's house and immediately she'd wanted to pee. Zeffirino had taken her to the toilet and shut her inside. Baby had spent a long time in there. The toilet was a simple hole cut into a board that people did their business in, which then dropped into the composting soil below. Beetles and little animals of all kinds would come crawling out of the hole and Baby was fascinated by them. We'd heard screams coming from the toilet, but we could no longer see Baby. She was so small that she'd fallen right through the hole.

'Baby, what are you doing down there?'

We just couldn't stop laughing.

I'd been left alone with Baby because the others had to help Pippone clean out the stables.

'Useless idiots!' Pippone was shouting.

We could hear the sound of the slaps he was giving Pasquetta. This noise was immediately followed by her screaming, followed by more slapping.

We were used to it so we knew nothing could be done and that we'd just have to play alone for the day.

I went out into the woods as usual to pick wild asparagus with Baby. From afar, we could hear the shouts of the soldiers who were staying at the Villa.

The noise of the birds had merged with the sound of the cannons, which grew louder every day. We went to see if the Madonna had visited.

'Look, a *caramelle*!' said Baby.

I bent down and saw that there really was a sweet on the ground. As I was bending over, I spotted another one not too far away.

'Another one!'

'I saw it first!'

'Fine, you can have it,' I said, having caught sight of a third a few metres away.

'It's the *miracolo delle caramelle*!' said Baby.

We suddenly heard a rustling sound. I looked up and saw a man with a beard sitting on a branch.

'Who are you? What's your name?'

'Giuseppe.'

'Like San Giuseppe!' said Baby.

I looked at his beard.

'Are you San Giuseppe?' Baby asked.

San Giuseppe nodded.

'Are you still hungry?' asked Baby, looking at the empty altar where only the bones of the chicken we had brought for the Madonna remained.

San Giuseppe nodded.

'We'll bring you some food,' said Baby.

'We'll even bring you dessert.'

San Giuseppe climbed down from the tree. He wanted to know about Uncle. Where was he? What was he doing? How many Germans were there at the Villa? What was their commander's name? He said he had come to save Uncle and that he wanted to talk to him.

Our skirts were full of cyclamens and mushrooms. San Giuseppe looked at Baby, then he lifted her onto his lap. He began to stroke her curls and kiss her. He squeezed her tight. I was sad not to be getting any kisses from San Giuseppe so I stepped forward.

'My turn,' I said.

San Giuseppe lifted me onto his right knee and kissed me too.

'Come back,' he said, as we were leaving to get him something to eat.

'I knew that San Giuseppe would appear before us one day.'

'You know, our Lady of Lourdes never kissed or hugged Bernadette.'

'That's true.'

'What I'd really like though is to get holy stigmata, like Saint Francis.'

I thought I'd heard the gong sound for dinner.

'It's late, dinner time.'

'We must thank the Madonna for sending us San Giuseppe.'

Before going home, we went round to tell Zeffirino that San Giuseppe was hungry.

'I'll give you San Giuseppe,' said Zeffirino's father, taking off his belt and chasing him to get back the loaf of bread Zeffirino had stolen. Baby and I hid behind a tree to watch.

But all that time Uncle had been sitting in the armchair waiting while Elsa fretted because no one was eating.

'We've been worried,' said Uncle. 'You're not allowed to go out at all tomorrow.'

We sat down at the table and Rosa began serving the food. When Uncle didn't speak it meant he was very angry. When I opened my mouth, Uncle told me to shut it.

'San Giuseppe is hungry!' Baby said to Elsa, as she was locking us in our room on Uncle's orders.

'Oh yeah, and where is he?'

'San Giuseppe is in the woods under the big oak tree and he's hungry. He's come to save uncle,' said Baby through the keyhole.

'The kind of stuff these two come up with! Soon the whole Holy Family will be over for dinner!'

'That's perjury!' Baby screamed with tears in her eyes.

Eventually Annie unlocked the door and came into the bedroom.

'Goodnight,' she said, slipping under the covers in her embroidered nightdress. 'No more talking.'

We'd put our nightdresses on over our dresses so we could go out in the middle of the night once Annie was asleep. Baby was crying and sucking on a sweet.

'Stop making noise!'

'Noise!' said the parrot they'd given us when our magpie had died from too much love. 'Not even Pedro can sleep!'

'Not even Pedro!'

Baby and I began to pray under our breath.

'*Chchchchchit aaaa-men,*' Pedro shrieked.

'Shhhh! Shut up!' Annie got up, turned on the light.

'Annie, I need to tell you something.'

'What is it?'

'Annie, what would you do if I told you that San Giuseppe was under the great oak tree and that he was hungry?'

'He is hungry!' Baby repeated.

'Annie, would you feed San Giuseppe who is hungry?'

'What are you talking about?'

'San Giuseppe is in the woods, waiting for Uncle.'

'You're telling lies!'

'No, it's not a lie! He came for Uncle. He came to save him!'

'It's true! It's true!' I was shouting, and I ran downstairs to tell Uncle.

Uncle was listening to the radio in the drawing room and seemed irritated by our intrusion.

Baby told him about San Giuseppe, who was in the woods and who had come to save him. She told Uncle that San Giuseppe was waiting for him under the big oak tree. Then Uncle said he would take care of San Giuseppe and agreed that San Giuseppe had undoubtedly come to save him. He said that he would take him food as long as we didn't say anything to anyone. This was a private matter between Uncle and San Giuseppe.

'If San Giuseppe really is in the woods, I'd better go to him right away.'

'But will you take him some food?' asked Baby.

'Of course I will take him some food.'

The following morning Uncle told us he had seen San Giuseppe.

'What did he say to you?' asked Baby.

'Not to tell anyone he was here.'

'I've been praying for you the whole time. That's why he came.'

Uncle hugged Baby and told her not to stop praying.

Uncle was looking out of the window at the woods in which San Giuseppe was hiding. At that moment, we heard a loud bang somewhere nearby. Baby ran over to the window.

'San Giuseppe must be scared!'

'Saints don't get scared,' said Uncle.

(38)

The roar of the cannons was closer than ever. The last of the soldiers' trucks were leaving the Villa under enemy fire. The air was full of whistling sounds and bullets were falling left and right like rain. What a thrill! We couldn't go out into the garden because Uncle wouldn't let us. Zeffirino and the others were all locked inside too, so they couldn't come out to play. Even the main road was deserted. For three days we'd not seen a single German soldier, nor a truck on the road that until then had been swarming with retreating troops.

Suddenly, even the firing of machine guns and the roar of the cannons ceased. There was a great calm. After a while, the peasants began to come out of their houses, shouting, 'The war is over! The Germans have gone! The partisans are on their way!'

A group of men with beards and rifles had appeared at the end of the avenue. Uncle went outside and ran towards them.

'Where's he going?' I asked Aunt Katchen. But Aunty didn't reply and watched from the window as Uncle took off with the partisans and disappeared into the woods.

Aunt Katchen hugged all three of us children tightly and burst into tears.

'Are you crying?' Baby asked.

'Yes, but with joy.'

So we went wild and started singing at the top of our lungs.

All of a sudden, we heard the sound of a truck.

'It's the English!' Katchen shouted, hurrying down the great staircase.

A car had stopped in front of the Villa. Soon after, a truck arrived, from which about twenty soldiers spilled out.

'Hainz!' said Baby. But then she realised that the soldiers were dressed differently from Hainz. They had badges on their hats and they all looked like officers.

'*Hauch, hauchauchauch!*' said two soldiers, lifting us both up.

'Let me go,' said Baby, squirming in his arms.

'*Hauchauchauch!*' said the soldier, squeezing me tight as I tried to wriggle free.

'Ouch! You're hurting me!' I said to the soldier who had caught me by the back of my dress, tearing it.

'*Hauchauchauch!*' he shouted.

'Look what you did!' I said, showing him my torn dress. 'You ripped it! You'll have to tell Elsa it was you!' I shouted angrily.

For a moment he looked confused but then he grabbed me again, kicking the dice we'd been playing with out of Baby's hands. Baby started to scream.

'*Haurauhauhauh!*' said another soldier, getting hold of Baby.

'Leave my little sister alone right this minute or I'll go and tell your commander.'

I saw Marie, Annie, and Katchen being driven up the stairs at gunpoint.

'Marie, Katchen!'

Then they were pushing us up the stairs of the Villa, too.

'You're rude!' Baby said.

'Yes, yes, you're a rude, nasty man! I'm going to tell the General and Hainz about you.'

They locked us all together in a room and left a sentry there to stand guard.

'Look what you've done to my Tro-tro,' Baby said, stroking the yellow bear she'd picked up off the floor. Somebody had stomped on its snout.

'You took his eye out!' she said, making a face.

Aunt Katchen called Baby over to her.

'Be good,' she said.

A little later an officer came in and asked where Uncle was. Once it became clear that none of us really knew, he left again.

Then the officer came back and asked us again in a few different languages.

We said we didn't know, but Baby said he'd gone to visit San Giuseppe.

Marie asked the sentry if Baby could go to the toilet. The sentry didn't answer.

'But I'm going to burst...' said Baby.

The sentry called another soldier over, who led Baby out with his machine gun pointed at her back. Before long the sentry opened the door and the same soldier led Baby in again.

We could hear banging and shouting and laughing. I could hear the sound of crystalware breaking, of chandeliers and mirrors being shattered. One clean strike and the piano was smashed.

'The piano!' Marie said.

Someone was going up and down the corridors on rollerskates and the whole house was shaking with the sounds of gunshots and boots. Someone kicked Alì, who started to whimper.

'They're hurting Alì!' Baby ran to the door to try and escape, but was shoved back.

'They're hurting Alì!' Annie started to cry.

Marie said, 'Don't cry.'

'Mamma,' Annie said, 'they're hurting Alì.'

Baby started hitting the guard with her clenched fists, pounding at his legs and screaming, 'Get off of me!'

To think of how often I'd been scolded by Uncle for breaking things like the big vase and the umbrella stand in the hall! To think of all the reprimands these soldiers would receive and the thousands of pages they'd have to fill out in their punishment journals if Uncle were here to see this!

I could tell exactly what was being broken by the noise the thing made as it fell to the floor, and which part of the Villa it was coming from. They were smashing the crystal glasses and bowls one at a time. You could hear roars of laughter accompanying each crash.

What would Uncle say to the Commander about the crystal glasses and his torn paintings and broken books when he got back?

They came to get us and took us downstairs to the salon to be questioned. Marie said it wasn't fair to treat us like that for no reason.

'Ah, but there'll be a fair trial,' said the Commander.

The mirrors were all broken. Some soldiers were roller skating around, screaming. Our toys were all over the place. The yellow bear had been shredded and stuck on top of a broomstick as a target. Baby insisted on picking up a ping-pong ball that had rolled between her feet. Glass covered the whole floor. A soldier, wearing one of Marie's floral shawls, was running up and down the staircase looking for the ball. He spotted it in Baby's hands. Baby held it out, frightened.

The white wall of the foyer was covered in scribbles and we could hear roars of laughter coming from the other rooms.

A soldier was coming down the great staircase, wearing a wide-brimmed ladies hat. I recognised it.

It was Aunt Katchen's. It was the one she kept for special occasions.

They pushed us into the salon and my feet stumbled over Uncle's books. All of the paintings on the walls had been slashed. It was almost dark and behind a table stood the Commander, the broken piano to his right. It was dark but the soldiers had brought torches.

The Commander smiled and bowed to Aunt Katchen.

'*Hyrhutyrhauh, jawohl,*' he said.

Then he translated what he'd said into French, to make sure us little ones could understand.

The Commander was a good man: he was smiling at us. He would give us a fair and proper trial, which in any case was just a formality. He asked us to please excuse him for what had happened and said he would question us one at a time, and then let us go right away.

Baby told the Commander about Alì, but the Commander didn't understand so Marie explained to him in German that Baby wanted Alì. The Commander smiled and ordered his troops not to touch Alì, and Annie said they should also not touch Pedro, and the Commander smiled and gave orders not to touch Pedro. Then they brought us back up to the room with the sentry.

'Now the trial can begin,' said the Commander and he smiled again and repeated that it was just a formality.

He sent for Aunt Katchen first, then a soldier came for Marie. After a while, he came back for Annie.

'Me too,' said Baby.

'Us too,' I said.

'No, not those two, they're not Jews.' And the sentry did not let us out.

We heard the firing of a machine gun, then a scream, then another gunshot, then another scream, then another gunshot.

Baby and I pushed past the sentry and rushed down the staircase, screaming, 'Marie! Katie! Annie!'

Soldiers were coming up the stairs. The door to the salon was open. It was red and lit by a torch. I thought I could make out their feet on the floor.

The Commander blocked the door, preventing us from going in. The soldiers pushed Baby and me outside. The peasants took us in their arms and led us away through the darkness. I turned around and saw flames flaring up. Suddenly the whole Villa was on fire. The peasants, all huddled together on the hill, watched as the Villa burned. They held us in their arms. Baby was in the farmer's arms and I was in Pippone's. Wails were coming from the Villa.

'It's them! They're burning!'

'No, it's the Germans leaving,' said Pippone and put his huge hand over my eyes. I strained my ears and heard the sound of the truck speeding away, the sound of its brakes as it headed down the hill.

'The Master!' Pippone cried.

Uncle was running downhill through the fields towards the Villa. The peasants threw themselves at him to try and stop him. Baby and I started running too, calling, 'Uncle Wilhelm!'

Behind him, a group of armed men were coming down from the woods.

Uncle was running towards the Villa, down the avenue after the German truck, screaming. He was dressed all in white and looked like a ghost.

The partisans caught up with Uncle and he crumbled to the ground.

Uncle Wilhelm was crying. I watched the bright headlights of the German trucks as they drove away into the distance.

Uncle was still with us.

'Uncle Wilhelm, Uncle Wilhelm!' Baby cried, hugging and kissing him. And I did the same, but he was crying that he wanted a gun. He was pleading for somebody to give him a gun because he wanted to die. But the men with beards and guns wouldn't give him one and I saw Uncle weep like a child.

'Why won't you give Uncle a gun!' I screamed.

'Give me your gun,' said Baby to one of the bearded men, beating him with her fists.

'Bad girls! You want to kill your uncle!' One shouted, bending over us.

'Not me, I don't want to kill Uncle.'

Baby started crying and so did I, and we kept hugging Uncle who was sitting on the ground and holding us tight, still calling for a gun and watching the flames as they rose up and illuminated us all as if it were daytime.

We stayed like that for hours and hours, Baby and I, watching the Villa burn, next to Uncle Wilhelm.

'Leave me alone, please leave me alone,' Uncle said to the peasants, who backed away slowly. The bearded men got into a car, saying they wanted to catch up with the Germans and kill them. They left one of their men behind to keep an eye on Uncle.

'Look after him!' their commander shouted.

Baby placed a hand over Uncle's eyes so that he would stop watching. But Uncle was trembling and kept watching the flames.

'Don't cry,' said Baby, hugging him. I was hugging him too.

'No,' said Uncle, 'Can't you see? I've stopped crying now.'

Baby fell asleep with her head on Uncle's lap, and I fell asleep, too, leaning against him as he watched the Villa burn.

I dreamt I was wandering through its empty corridors, through an infinity of wide-open doors that led into rooms in which there were no people. There was nobody at all, and I was afraid.

Then I woke up. Uncle was gone.

(39)

It was almost dawn. The Villa was smouldering. Baby and I entered the Villa. The broken mirrors reflected the light from the sky which poured in through the slats of the burned roof.

They were all there. Uncle too.

Baby bent down to look at Uncle and got blood on her dress.

'Are you sleeping?' Baby said to Uncle.

She leaned over Marie.

'Marie?' she said, 'Aunt Katchen?'

Baby was crouching over Uncle. She was talking to him.

'He's not answering. They're not answering.' She began to cry and scream, wiping her tears away with her bloodied hands. So I began to cry and scream too.

Then the peasants came in and took us away.

Dear Baby, dear Penny,

Remember me and Katchen and Annie and Marie, and the lessons Katchen and I have taught you. Forgive me if I have been a little boring and sometimes too strict. I'm thinking of you and hugging you tight.

Your Uncle WILHELM

P.S. Please don't wear mourning.

When Pippone brought us the note that they had found next to Uncle, Baby and I burst into tears again. The peasant women had washed their bodies. Vittorio had made coffins from wood salvaged from the doors of the Villa. The women were praying and wailing, saying, 'Jesus, Jesus, take them to Heaven with you...'

'But the Master committed suicide, and suicide is a sin, so he can't be buried in the cemetery with our dead. His wife and girls, yes, they were baptised, but he didn't believe in God, he wasn't a Christian, nor baptised neither...'

'He never went to Mass.'

'And you can't bury the Master and there's no place in the cemetery for suicides...'

'You have to get permission from the Bishop...'

'And who's gonna go and find the Bishop in all this cannon fire!'

'It ain't even a nice coffin, poor Master. Him, he could've had a fancy one: zinc on the inside, walnut on the outside... But I did me best, ain't that the truth, young ladies?' and he turned to us. Baby started crying even louder, and I held onto her tight.

At that moment, the priest rushed in, quite out of breath. Baby clung to his cassock.

The peasant women stood up, weeping and wailing. One of the old women said, 'We ain't gonna let him lie among our dead.'

'Why?' asked the priest, continuing to hold Baby and me.

''Cus he ain't Christian and he's a suicide...'

The priest stood in thought for a moment.

'You have to get permission from the Bishop,' the peasants said.

Pierino and Zeffirino entered, their arms overflowing with flowers. They walked over the broken glass.

The priest lowered Baby onto the ground and asked, 'Are the oxen ready?'

'Yes, Father,' said Pippone.

'Let's go then.'

'Where to?'

'To the cemetery, to bury them.'

'What about the Master?'

'The Master, too.'

The priest got the peasants to hoist the coffins onto the cart, but they refused to bury Uncle in the cemetery. So the priest set off alone, driving the oxcart down the hill.

The priest had already disappeared round the bend and out of sight before Pippone took the first step in the direction of the cemetery. The men followed behind him, and behind them came the women, who were taking it in turns to carry Baby.

The priest was praying.

Baby walked up to him, 'Is Uncle going to Hell?'

'Hell doesn't exist but for the wicked,' the priest said.

The peasants wanted to take us away, but they had to tear us from the burial mound with force.

'We're staying here!' said Baby, shouting.

'We're staying here. Right here with them!' I said, clinging to the earth. Then I began to scream.

(41)

Baby and I were in the cemetery.

'Don't cry, Baby.'

'I'll stop crying if you stop crying.'

'Look, I'm not crying anymore,' I said, wiping my eyes.

Baby leaned over the tomb and called out, 'Annie? Marie?' She pressed her ear to the ground.

Then she started crying again.

'They can't hear me!'

Still crying, she lifted her head. Her eyes widened, 'Look, it's Don Quixote!'

Don Quixote de la Mancha was standing before us at the cemetery gate.

Skinny and lank, he was wearing his flat tin cap. His long bare legs were sticking out of his shorts.

But where was Sancho Panza?

Don Quixote was alone. He advanced as if he were riding against the windmills, looking all around him with caution. He looked at us, a little surprised. Then he smiled the sweet smile of Don Quixote.

'Hello,' he said in English, coming forward with his lance in his hand. He had branches on his head. As he bent over Baby, there was a metallic clang, and it looked as if he were about to snap in two.

'Hello, are there any Germans around?' he asked.

His face was covered in freckles.

'Hello,' said Baby, giving a little cursty and wiping away her tears.

Don Quixote brought his freckled face closer to Baby.

'And who are you?' he asked.

'I am Baby and this is my sister,' said Baby, curtsying again.

Don Quixote looked at Baby and me and said something I didn't understand. He took some sweets out from the pocket of his shirt. Then he walked back into the bushes on his long legs.

He turned back several times to wave at us, 'Bye bye!'

Baby started running down the path, falling, then getting back up again.

I dedicate this novel to my uncle, Robert Einstein, cousin to Albert; to my aunt, Nina Mazzetti Einstein, and my cousins, Annamaria (Cicci) and Luce Einstein. They all sleep in the Badiuzza cemetery near Florence, between San Donato, on the hill, and Rignano sull'Arno. Their tombstone reads: 'Murdered by the Germans on August 3rd, 1944'.

My sister and I, who had lived at the Villa since we were children (because our mother had died), were spared by the SS because our name was not Einstein but Mazzetti.

We shared the joys of life with them and received their affection for years but we were separated in death. This life was gifted to me only because I was 'of another race'.

All survivors carry the weight of this 'privilege', along with the need to bear witness.

This book attempts to describe the joy and happiness that their family gave me during my childhood, welcoming me as an "equal," though I was only "equal" to them in joy and "different" at the moment of death. They sleep there on the hill and I remember them. If you happen to pass by, leave a flower.

Roma – May 1993

This edition was published by Another Gaze Editions in 2022 www.anothergazeeditions.com

ISBN: 978 1 3999 3735 1

Originally published in Italy by Sellerio Editore Palermo Copyright © 1993
Copyright in the foreword: © Ali Smith
Copyright in the introduction: © Francesca Massarenti
All rights reserved.

The right of Lorenza Mazzetti to be identified as the author of this work has been asserted in accordance with Section 77 of the Copyright, Designs and Patent Act 1988.

1 2 3 4 5 6 7 8 9 10
Translation: Livia Franchini
Design: Virginie Gauthier
Typeset in Epicene Text
Printing: PBtisk a.s (CZ)

Daniella Shreir and Missouri Williams (Another Gaze Editions) would like to thank Brighid Lowe and Henry K Miller for sharing their insights into the life and work of Lorenza Mazzeti, and offering their support from the beginning to the completion of this project. Thank you in particular to Brighid, who facilitated the publication of Mazzetti's drawings.

This book has been translated thanks to a translation grant awarded by the Italian Ministry of Foreign Affairs and International Cooperation.